BEAKY MALONE

MALONE

WORLD'S GREATEST LIAR

For Moira – for all the babysitting and Boxing
Day dinners ... and for not shouting at me
when I made your lights explode ~ BH

For The Guy with the Hat and our furry son,
Baron Francis Squiggleface (the third) ~ Katie Abey

STRIPES PUBLISHING LIMITED
An imprint of Little Tiger Group
1 Coda Studios, 189 Munster Road,
London SW6 6AW

Imported into the EEA by Penguin Random House Ireland,
Morrison Chambers, 32 Nassau Street, Dublin D02 YH68

A paperback original
First published in Great Britain in 2016

Text copyright © Barry Hutchison, 2016
Illustrations copyright © Katie Abey, 2016

ISBN: 978-1-78895-577-5

The right of Barry Hutchison and Katie Abey to be identified as the author and illustrator
of this work has been asserted by them in accordance with the Copyright, Designs and
Patents Act, 1988.

A CIP catalogue record for this book is available from the British Library.

Printed and bound in the UK.

The Forest Stewardship Council® (FSC®) is a global, not-for-profit organization
dedicated to the promotion of responsible forest management worldwide. FSC®
defines standards based on agreed principles for responsible forest stewardship that
are supported by environmental, social, and economic stakeholders. To learn more, visit
www.fsc.org

10 9 8 7 6 5 4 3 2 1

BEAKY MALONE

MALONE

WORLD'S GREATEST LIAR

BARRY HUTCHISON

ILLUSTRATED BY KATIE ABEY

LITTLE TIGER
LONDON

CHAPTER 1

MEET BEAKY

Theo heaved his bag higher on his shoulder and shot me a doubting look.

"You don't believe me, do you?" I said.

He shook his head. "That you've been asked to go on an expedition to the North Pole?" he snorted. "No, Beaky, not really."

I pulled a wounded face. "That hurts, Theo," I said. "Considering you're meant to be my best friend, that really hurts." I took a deep breath. "But you're right. I haven't been asked to go on an expedition to the North Pole."

BEAKY
WOZ
ERE

HEY

"Knew it," Theo said.

"I've been asked to *lead* the expedition."

"Oh, *right*," Theo replied. "Well, that's much more believable."

"Apology accepted," I said, as we rounded the corner leading on to our street. Theo lived three doors down from me, and we'd walked to and from school together since Reception class. We'd been the same height when we'd started, but these days he towered above me like a beanpole.

"I didn't apologize!" Theo grumbled.

"You apologized in your mind," I said. "Trust me. I'm moderately psychic."

"Course you are,"

Theo laughed. "What number am I thinking of?"

I tapped the side of my head with a finger. "Four."

Theo's eyes widened a little, then he shook his head. "Lucky guess."

"I knew you were going to say that," I told him. He grinned. "You're such a liar, Beaky."

"How dare you, sir!" I said, raising my fists. "Do you know what happened to the last person who called me a liar?"

"Yeah, nothing," Theo said. "It was me earlier this morning when you said that eating jam made dogs explode."

"It does!" I protested. "I read it in a book."

We stopped outside Theo's house. "Anyway, what about you?" I asked. "What are you up to this weekend?"

"Well, I can't compete with visiting the North Pole," Theo admitted. "So I'll probably just play Xbox and eat crisps."

I nodded. "Usual, then."

He vaulted over his gate and into his garden. "Pretty much. Enjoy the snow, Beaky. Watch out for polar bears."

"Oh, I'm not doing it," I said. "They wanted me to wear a jacket, so I said no. I never wear jackets."

"You're wearing one now," Theo pointed out.

"This is a waterproof coat," I said. "They're two very different things, Theo. Everyone knows that."

Theo laughed. "I stand corrected. See you tomorrow, then?"

"You provide the Xbox, I'll bring the crisps," I said. We did our complicated farewell handshake, which neither of us really knew how to do properly, then said our goodbyes. I grinned the rest of the way home. Xbox and crisps. This was going to be a brilliant weekend.

Or so I thought.

"So," said Mum, looking round the dinner table. "How did everyone's day go?"

Mum was smiling at us far more enthusiastically than usual. That, combined with the fact she'd made us a massive fry-up – which she only did on special occasions – told me something was up. I watched her closely, trying to figure out what it might be, but Mum could be pretty cagey when she wanted to be.

Dad smiled. "Today, I wrote a song about..."

He did a drumroll on the table with his fingers. "Toilet paper," he announced. He dipped a chip in his fried egg and sat back. "I know, I know, I can tell you're very impressed, but please … no autographs."

"Toilet paper? I bet it stinks," I said, grinning proudly at what was clearly an excellent joke. No one else seemed to get it, though.

"You take that back, Dylan," said Mum, using my real name as always. "Your dad works very hard writing his silly little tunes to put food on this table."

"Silly little tunes?"  said Dad, gasping and clutching at his chest. "I've never been so insulted!"

Mum waved a hand dismissively. "You know what I mean."

Dad shrugged. "Yeah, fair enough."

She had a point, I suppose. Still, I wasn't convinced Dad worked *that* hard. The last jingle he'd written had been for a dog-food advert, and just went "Woof, woof, woof, woof, woof, woof," over and over again.

"Sorry, Dad," I said. "I'm sure your song's great."

Dad shook his head. "Oh, it isn't. It's terrible. But thanks, anyway."

"What about you, Jodie?" said Mum.

All eyes went to my sister who was slowly shoving beans around her plate with her fork. She looked up and tugged an earphone out of her ear. "What?"

"How was your day?" said Mum.

"All right," she shrugged, then she put the earphone back in.

Mum kept smiling at her, expecting more. It didn't come.

"OK, then!" she said, turning to me. "Dylan?"

"I fought a swan."

Mum blinked. Clearly, she hadn't been expecting that. She glanced across to Dad, who rolled his eyes in response.

"Right, well. A productive day all round then," Mum said. She cleared her throat nervously, then reached over and tugged Jodie's earphones out.

"Hey!" Jodie protested.

"I got a bit of good news today," Mum announced, smiling far too broadly for it to be natural now. "Aunt Jas is coming to visit!"

Dad gasped.

Jodie groaned.

I spluttered into my glass, spraying orange juice up both nostrils. It was surprisingly refreshing.

"*What?*" asked Dad. "What do you mean, "Aunt Jas is coming to visit'?"

Aunt Jas is my aunt. The clue's in the name, really. She's Mum's sister, and a bit like Mum, only younger, darker-haired and much, much louder. The last time she'd visited had been over a year ago, and we were only now starting to recover from the ordeal.

Aunt Jas is a little bit ... full on. She speaks at 100% volume all the time, and has a way of screaming when she laughs that sounds like fingernails being dragged down a blackboard. She and Mum always manage to rub each other up the wrong way, and are constantly trying to outdo one another. Her last visit had ended in them having a full-scale screaming match in the cinema. In front of 200 people. During the film.

I doubted Mum was looking forward to the visit, but she was doing her best to put a brave face on it. She popped a chip in her mouth and gave a shrug as she chewed. "I mean Jas is coming. For the weekend. Her and Steve and—"

"Not the kids," said Dad, his eyes widening in horror. "Please, not the kids."

"Of course she's bringing the kids," Mum tutted. "What else would she do with them?"

"Sell them to the zoo?" muttered Jodie.

"That's no way to talk about your cousins," Mum snapped. She was getting annoyed. Any minute now she'd start tapping her foot. Any minute after that, she'd explode. The tension needed to be defused and fast. Time to deploy some Beaky charm.

I blew the juice out of my nostrils and set my glass down on the table. "Well, I think it'll be nice having them here."

Dad and Jodie stared at me in disbelief. Even Mum blinked in surprise. "You've told some whoppers in your time, Beaky," said Jodie. "But that's got to be the biggest yet."

"Stop calling your brother 'Beaky'," said Mum.

"Everyone calls him Beaky."

"Well, they shouldn't," Mum said, leaning over and giving my hand a comforting squeeze. "It's not his fault he's got a massive nose."

"I wouldn't say it's massive," I protested.

Jodie nodded. "It is. It's proper massive."

"It's statuesque," I said.

"It's *elephant*esque, more like."

I flicked my fork, firing a ketchup-coated chip in Jodie's direction. She ducked at the last moment, and our Great Dane, Destructo, leaped up from the floor and snatched it out of the air. It was a bit like a scene from *Jurassic Park*, but with a dog instead of a dinosaur, and a chip instead of a screaming tourist. While Destructo isn't quite as big as a T-rex, his appetite is pretty similar.

"Hey!" yelled Jodie, snatching up a wobbly fistful of egg.

Dad held his hands up for calm. "Cut it out, you two," he cried. "Everyone just calm down. Stop throwing food. Stop going on about Beaky's massive great nose and let's deal with the problem at hand."

He waited for Jodie to put her egg back on

her plate (which she did, much to Destructo's disappointment), then took a bite of sausage. "Now," he said, chewing thoughtfully. "When are they coming?"

"Tonight," said Mum.

Now it was Dad's turn to choke. He seemed to inhale the sausage in one sharp breath. His eyes went wide and he frantically thudded at his chest, coughing and spluttering in panic.

"Stand back, I know the Heimlich manoeuvre," I announced, leaping up from the table. I didn't really know the Heimlich, obviously, but I'd seen someone do it on telly once and it didn't look all that difficult.

Wrapping my arms round him from behind, I heaved my dad to his feet. It turns out he's heavier than he looks, though, and I immediately toppled backwards, pulling him down with me. We hit the ground with a *thud* and an *oof*. The sudden impact launched the lump of sausage high into the air, where it was immediately caught by a delighted Destructo, who had no trouble swallowing it at all.

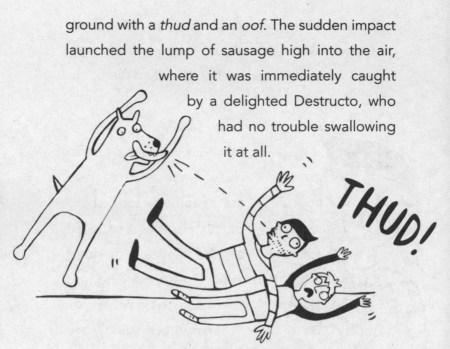

THUD!

Jodie leaned over the table and peered down at us. "So, that was the Heimlich, was it?"

"Advanced Heimlich," I wheezed as Dad rolled off me. "Just something I invented."

"Tonight?" Dad yelped, finally finding his voice. "Why are they coming tonight?"

"Wasps," said Mum.

Jodie, Dad and I all looked at one another.

"Everyone else heard her say 'wasps' there, right?" I asked.

"They've got a wasps' nest," Mum explained.

"They're not bringing it, are they?" I asked.

Mum tutted. "Don't be silly, Dylan. It's in their house. They can't get anyone to deal with it until Monday."

Dad's face went a funny shade of purple. "Monday? They're not staying until Monday, are they?"

"Of course not," said Mum. Dad seemed to relax a little, but it didn't last long. "They're staying till Tuesday."

"WHAT?!" cried Dad.

Mum smirked. "Not really. They're going home on Sunday."

Dad sat down in his seat and shifted uncomfortably. He looked at the rest of his sausage, then pushed the plate away. I knew how he felt. Aunt Jas's visit meant I could kiss goodbye to Xbox and crisps with Theo.

"I suppose it might not be that bad," Dad said. "It's only a couple of days."

"That's the spirit," said Mum, but she looked just as ashen-faced as Dad did. "And who knows? It might even be fun," she added.

"Fun?" Dad spluttered. He forced a smile. "I mean … fun. Yeah. Fun. You might be right."

As it turned out, though, she wasn't.

CHAPTER 2

AUNT JAS

We had cleared away the dinner plates and were all chipping away at slabs of a Wall's Viennetta (the minty one) when the doorbell rang. Destructo sprang to his feet and began barking his head off. Dad looked across at Mum and managed a thin smile.

"Here goes, then."

"Here goes," said Mum. She reached over and squeezed his hand.

The doorbell rang again. Destructo barked louder. "Better let them in, I suppose," Mum said.

No one moved.

"Yep," agreed Dad.

Still no one moved.

The doorbell rang for a third time. Destructo kept barking, but now he was shooting us a sideways glance, like he was concerned we'd all gone deaf. The tension was killing me, so before the bell could ring yet again, I jumped to my feet. "I'll get it, then, shall I?" I said.

The moment I turned the lock, Aunt Jas threw the door wide open, almost knocking me off my feet.

"TA-DAAA!"

she cried, like a magician who'd just done a really impressive trick. "We're heeeere!"

This only made Destructo worse. He began racing in circles, barking and howling at nobody in particular. Aunt Jas glanced at him warily as she reached for my face. "Oh, look how big you're getting!" she said, her glossy red lips puckering up for a kiss.

"I wouldn't," I warned. "I've got the Brown Death."

Jas faltered. "What's the Brown Death?"

"It's like the Black Death, only not quite as bad," I explained. "I'd keep my distance if I were you."

Frowning, Jas looked over at Mum. "Is he being serious?"

Mum shook her head. "No."

Jas's face lit up. "Aah! You almost got me! Come here, you." I was suddenly surrounded by a cloud of perfume as Jas caught me in a bear hug and planted a big wet kiss on my forehead.

Over her shoulder, three more shapes shambled in through the door – two little ones followed by one big one.

How can I describe my cousins, Sophie and Max? Well, one's called Sophie and one's called Max, obviously. Sophie's a couple of years younger than me, and is OK in a doesn't-actually-do-anything-interesting sort of way. Mum would never admit it, but  Sophie creeps us all out because she hardly ever says anything, and just sort of stares all the time.

Max, on the other hand, isn't creepy so much as plain horrible. He's seven, likes loud noises and spectacular violence, and is probably part demon. When he's not hitting people for no reason, he's pulling the legs off insects, chasing cats or breaking anything that takes his fancy. He loves causing trouble, but Jas and Steve never seem to tell him off for anything. Last time they were here he poured orange juice into the stereo, completely destroying it. Jas and Steve laughed it off as "a bit of fun".

Max is also completely selfish, which was why he now made a beeline for my mum's dessert and started tucking into it without even saying hello.

"Don't mind him," said Jas. "He's a growing lad. He's just hungry."

"He doesn't look hungry," I heard Dad mutter, but the sound of Destructo's barking covered for him. He was right, though. While Sophie was small and skinny for her age, Max looked about three burgers away from becoming a perfect sphere.

Steve stumbled in, staggering beneath the weight of the luggage he was carrying. He and Aunt Jas have been together for nearly fifteen years, but Steve has always refused to get married, claiming it's "totally uncool". Mum says he's just scared of commitment, but Dad reckons he's probably more scared of Aunt Jas.

Whatever the reason, I'd overheard Mum say Jas was getting fed up of him trying to weasel out of marriage, and that they'd been arguing about it a lot lately. So that was something to look forward to…

I saw Dad's face go tight when he spotted how many bags Steve was carrying, but he bit his lip and didn't say anything about it.

"Where do you want these, cutie-smoosh?" Steve asked. He was wearing sunglasses, despite the fact it was raining outside. Then again, from what I remembered of Steve, he always wore sunglasses, even in the house.

Jodie and I looked at one another. "Cutie-smoosh?" we mouthed, silently.

"Anywhere," said Jas, without turning round. Her voice was clipped, and I guessed Steve must be in the doghouse for something.

Speaking of dogs...

"Destructo! Shut up!" Jodie bellowed.

Destructo immediately stopped barking and rolled over on to his back. Jodie's the only person in the family he ever listens to, probably because she's the scariest. "Hi, Aunt Jas," Jodie said, having a bash at something resembling a smile.

She stood up and gave Jas the briefest of brief hugs, then sat back down again. By the time she'd done that, Max was halfway through her ice cream and already eyeing up mine. I put my arms round my bowl.

"I've sneezed on it," I told him, meeting his gaze. "Twice. On purpose."

The next few minutes went by in a flurry of "hello's" and "so good to see you's" and "you're looking well's." Max finished all the available puddings, kicked the table as he left the dining area, then threw himself down on the sofa and turned on the TV. Jas hugged us all several more times, while still giving Steve the cold shoulder, and Sophie hung about at the edge of the room, quietly freaking everyone out.

The few minutes after that were spent in awkward silence and, within half an hour of Jas arriving, the strain was already starting to show.

We had left the dining end of the front room and were now in the living area, sitting on the sofas and perched on the arms. Max had moved over to Dad's armchair and was sprawled on it, upside down, watching cartoons. Dad kept giving him a dirty look, but Max was too engrossed in the telly to notice.

"So, I'm guessing you haven't planned anything for the weekend?" said Jas, ever so slightly accusingly.

Mum's whole body stiffened. "I have, actually," she replied.

Jas raised an eyebrow. "Oh? What?"

Mum hesitated. "It's a secret," she said, eventually.

"A secret?"

Mum nodded. "Yep."

Jas smiled. "It's OK if you haven't. We're happy just slobbing around here like you lot."

"Slobbing?" said Mum. "What's that supposed to mean?"

I leaned over the back of the sofa, getting between them before things could kick off. "You may as well tell them, Mum," I said. She looked at me blankly. "About the trip you've organized. With the castle visit and all that stuff."

"Oh ... yes. The castle visit," Mum said, almost laughing with relief. "Well, I guess the secret's out."

"And the trip to the high-wire adventure park on Sunday," I added. I saw Mum's eyes narrow, and quickly put an arm round her shoulders. "I've been asking to go for months," I told Jas, "but she's always said it's too expensive. Not for you guys, though. 'Nothing's too good for Aunt Jas and her family.' That's what you said, isn't it, Mum?"

Mum gritted her teeth and forced a smile. "Yes, that's what I said."

"And you said you'd raise my pocket money," I continued, giving her shoulders a squeeze.

She shot me a sideways glance. "Don't push it."

"Well, that sounds just awesome," said Steve from behind his mirrored lenses. He gave a double thumbs up which he must've thought was cool, but was just a bit embarrassing, really. "Doesn't it, kids?"

COOL

"No," said Max loudly. Sophie just stared in eerie silence from across the room.

"As long as we don't have to rely on you to give directions," said Jas, flashing an insincere smile. "We might never find it."

Steve sighed. "Come on, cutie-smoosh, it was one wrong turn."

"It was four wrong turns. One of them into a field. We'd have been here ages ago had it not been for your navigating."

Dad leaned closer to me. "I knew I liked Steve," he whispered. Mum shot him an angry look that shut him right up.

"It wasn't my fault – Max had drawn all over the map!" Steve protested.

Aunt Jas was still smiling, but the strain of keeping it in place was beginning to show. "He drew a dinosaur, and you tried to navigate round it," she said. "Did you really think there was a whole area marked 'Here Be Dragons' off the M4?"

"Not off the M4," I chipped in, "but Junction 12 of the M6 used to be heaving with dragons, back in the day. Of course, they didn't call it the M6 then, because numbers hadn't been invented. They called it 'Ye Olde Dragon's Road'. Because of all the dragons," I added helpfully.

Everyone stared at me in silence. Especially Sophie, who stared at me in silence twice as hard as everyone else.

"Well, if you'd just let me use the satnav like a normal person, it wouldn't matter what was drawn on the map, would it?" Jas said.

 "Where's the fun in that?" asked Steve, trying to laugh the situation off.

"You call that journey fun?" seethed Jas.

"Right," said Dad, leaping to his feet and startling everyone. "I'm off to bed."

Mum looked up at him. "What? But it's barely seven-thirty."

"Is it? Already? Blimey. No wonder I'm so tired," he said, stepping over the tangle of legs around the coffee table. "Night, everyone!"

He faked a yawn, then darted out of the room.

And to think people had the cheek to call me a liar! I'd never stoop as low as that.

Or would I?

I stretched, faked a much more convincing yawn, then got to my feet. "I think I might get an early night, too. My bed is calling."

"Um yes, about that," said Mum. She glanced across to Jodie, who was staring intently at her phone. "You and Jodie are going to have to share."

Jodie's head snapped up. "What? Why?"

"For space. Jas, Steve and the kids can take Dylan's room, and Dylan can sleep on your floor."

"No, I can't," I pointed out. "I've got a bad back."

"No, you haven't." Jodie shot me one of her Looks. She's got a lot of different Looks, none of them good. This was her "Don't push it" Look, but I wasn't about to let that stop me.

"I have," I replied. "I jarred it playing football at school last week. The nurse thinks it's a herniated disc, so I'm afraid I'll have to take the bed."

Mum's eyes narrowed in suspicion. "Why didn't you say anything?"

"Because you've got enough on your mind, Mum," I said, resting my hand on top of hers. "The last thing I wanted to do was worry you."

"You are not getting the bed," Jodie growled.

"Well, I am," I said. "Firstly because of my bad back, and secondly because I can run faster."

With that I raced out of the room, took the stairs two at a time and hurled myself on to Jodie's bed.

CHAPTER 3

THE CASTLE TRIP

I'll be honest – I slept like a log and woke up feeling very refreshed the next morning. The same couldn't be said for Jodie, who woke up looking like an extra from a zombie movie. Her hair was knotted, there was drool on her cheek and she hobbled about like she'd aged eighty years overnight.

"I'll get you for this, Beaky," she warned, as I

skipped past her out of the room. "I've had it with your lies. You need to stop."

"OK," I said.

Jodie blinked. "Really?"

I stuck my tongue out. "Nah. That was a lie, too. Good, eh?"

I ducked round the door as she chucked a shoe at me, then slid down the banister and strolled into the living room.

At breakfast, I had great fun making up stories about how Jodie had spent the night snoring and talking about boys from her class. Jodie tried to punch me under the table, but accidentally thumped a very unimpressed Dad instead.

After we'd cleared away the breakfast stuff, we all piled into Aunt Jas's seven-seater car. Considering there were eight of us, this wasn't easy. We had to bring Destructo along, too, because whenever he's left alone he tries to eat the TV. I was wedged into one of the back seats between Jodie, who kept digging her elbows into me, and Sophie, who I caught staring at me whenever I glanced her way.

Dad and Steve were up front, while Mum and Jas sat on the two seats behind them. Jas had Max on her knee and was holding him in place with a complicated armlock.

"So ... is everyone ready to have some fun?" asked Mum, as Steve guided the car out of the driveway and on to the main road.

Jas shrugged. "I'm sure it'll be fine. We've got a castle near us which is bigger, so... I'm sure it'll be fine, though."

"This one's older," said Mum.

"Queen Victoria once stayed at ours," Jas retorted.

Mum looked crestfallen. How could she compete with that?

"Queen Victoria *built* this one," I said, leaping to her aid, "with her bare hands."

I gave Mum a sly wink. She sighed, but smiled with it. "Well, I don't think that's quite true," she said, "but it's still an impressive castle."

Dad made a sudden dive for the radio. "Ooh, ooh, turn it up, this is one of mine."

Jodie and I groaned. Dad had written dozens of radio jingles over the years and whenever he heard one he insisted on singing along. The more ridiculous the lyrics, the more he seemed to enjoy it. Which was handy, because all of the lyrics were ridiculous.

He took a deep breath. The music swelled. He opened his mouth and...

"Ifffff **yooooou've got a stingy botty, that's looking red and spotty, then don't let it drive you dotty any mooooore!**"

"Dad!" Jodie said. "Please. No one wants to hear you singing about butt cream.

"Steve raised his hand. "Dude! I totally want to hear you singing about butt cream."

"Thank you, Steve," said Dad triumphantly. He looked back over his shoulder. "Second verse, same as the first. **Ifffff yoooou've...**"

Jodie and I sank deeper into our seats. Even Destructo gave a whine from the boot. This was going to be a very long drive.

What felt like hours later, but which was actually just twenty agonizing minutes or so, the humans in our group stood outside Piddington Castle, looking up at its moss-coated walls. Destructo, meanwhile, was locked in the car with the windows left open, under strict instructions not to destroy anything.

My class had done a project on Piddington Castle the year before, although we hadn't been allowed to actually visit it in case we somehow found a way to knock it down. I remembered the teacher had made it sound like a pretty exciting place, but I'd completely forgotten all the details. Still, I wasn't about to let that stop me.

"Of course, it was originally called *Piggington Castle*," I said. "Because the first family to live here was actually a family of pigs. Not many people know that."

"Because it isn't true," Jodie said.

"It is. I did a project on it at school."

Mum leaned past me to look at Jodie. "He did do a project on it at school. I remember."

"Oh well, then it *must* be true," Jodie tutted.

"It was also originally built of solid gold, but cars kept crashing because the gold dazzled the drivers."

"They didn't have cars back then, did they?" Steve frowned.

"They did round here," I said proudly. "We've always been very advanced in these parts."

"Aaaaaargh! You're driving me crazy. Just stop!"

Jodie cried. She crammed her earphones in her ears and crossed her arms, signalling she wanted nothing more to do with any of us for the rest of the day.

I rolled my eyes and gave an amused shake of the head. "Teenagers, eh?"

Aunt Jas looked up at the castle. "It's not very big, is it?" she said.

"It's bigger on the inside," I assured her. "Like the TARDIS in *Doctor Who*. Now," I said, gesturing towards the castle's unimpressive-looking front door. "Shall we?"

We found out there was a battle re-enactment taking place in the castle grounds, so we hung around with half a dozen other people to watch that. I'd never seen a battle re-enactment before, but it wasn't quite what I expected. I'd been hoping for hundreds of actors all bashing each other to bits, but it turned out to be two blokes in chainmail armour running around in circles and vaguely swinging at each other with fake swords. The ground was quite muddy so they kept falling over, which was funny the first six or seven times, but the joke began to wear thin pretty quickly after that.

Even my fascinating-and-fun trivia about the history of the battle wasn't enough to keep everyone interested. Just after I'd told them about how one side of the conflict had successfully rallied an army of bees to help them, they all decided to go for a look around inside.

44

I'm the first to admit that the outside of the castle was not that impressive, but inside was a different story. Inside was *really* unimpressive.

The floor was grey. The walls were grey. The ceiling was grey. The sky outside was overcast, which meant the windows also looked grey. There was an occasional tapestry hanging on the wall, but even those had faded away to shades of charcoal. It felt more like being inside a pencil drawing of a castle than inside a real one.

The castle guides (who wore grey uniforms and mostly had grey hair) looked almost as bored as everyone else. They wandered around with their hands behind their backs, loudly sighing whenever anyone asked them a question.

"Well ... this is nice," said Mum, smiling hopefully. "Isn't it?"

"It's rubbish," said Max. He had a finger up his nose all the way to the second knuckle, and was rummaging around like he might strike gold up there. "It's boring."

"Now, now, Max, that's not nice," Jas scolded. "Your aunt has worked very hard to arrange this for us." Jas glanced around, then looked over at Mum. "He's right, though. It is rubbish. Why did you bring us here?"

Mum turned and shot me a very deliberate look. "Yes, remind me, Dylan – why did I bring us here?"

It was a very good question. I'd always wanted to visit the castle since doing our school project, but now I was here I had absolutely no idea why.

"Because it's haunted, of course," I announced, thinking fast.

Max's finger paused, mid-rummage. He glanced along the castle corridor in both directions. "Cool."

Steve's face lit up. "Haunted? Oh man, that's awesome. You mean, like, with ghosts?"

"No, Steve, with monkeys," Jas snapped. She was still angry with Steve, and I was beginning to suspect the problem was bigger than his lack of map-reading skills. The marriage issue, I guessed. "Of course with ghosts. What else would it be haunted with?"

"Actually," I said, "one of the ghosts *is* a baboon. Which, while not technically a monkey, is pretty closely related, so—"

"A ghostly baboon?" Jodie snapped, raising her voice over the music only she could hear. "In a gold castle that used to be run by pigs? Do you even listen to the words that come out of your mouth, Beaky?"

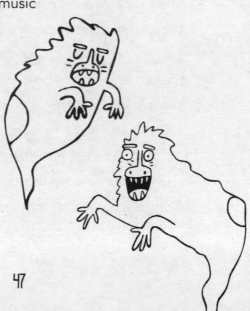

47

"No, but only because I'm self-deaf," I said. "Meaning I can hear everything except the sound of my own voice."

Jodie gritted her teeth. "Argh! Shut up!"

"It's a terrible affliction and I'm hurt you'd choose to make fun of it," I said.

Before Jodie could say anything else, Aunt Jas spun on the spot. "Where are Max and Sophie?"

Everyone looked around, except Jodie, who kept glaring at me and cracking her knuckles. Max and Sophie were nowhere to be seen.

"Oh no! What if the ghosts got them?" said Steve. I glanced at him, not sure if he was joking. With his sunglasses on, it was difficult to tell.

"I've got tracking experience," I said. "I once tracked an ant from one end of town to the other. When it was raining."

"No, he didn't," said Dad.

"Well, I did, I just didn't tell you about it. If anyone can find them, I can," I said, setting off along the corridor. "I'll be back in no time. You stay here in case they come back. Just relax and admire all the … grey."

It didn't take an expert tracker to find Max and Sophie. There were only two doors leading off from the corridor and one of them was locked. I followed the next passageway for a few metres, then stopped and listened.

Any second now…

CRASH!

Yep, that was bound to be Max. I set off towards the sound and found my cousins standing over a fallen suit of armour. They were in a dimly lit room which was cordoned off by a length of red rope. I glanced around, then ducked under the rope and joined them. They both looked up, surprised to see me.

We clearly weren't supposed to be in there, so I closed the heavy wooden door behind me, plunging the room into a gloomy half-darkness.

"It was like that when we got here," insisted Max, pointing to the scattered armour.

"Was it?" I said. "Then maybe it was knocked over by the Piddington Phantom."

Max frowned. "The what?"

"The Piddington Phantom," I whispered, glancing nervously into the shadows for dramatic effect. "Legend has it the phantom stalks the corridors of this very castle, always on the look-out for trespassers."

Sophie swallowed. "T-trespassers?"

Hey, she could talk! That was a turn-up for the books.

I nodded solemnly. "The younger the better. It scuttles through the shadows like a spider, sniffing out those who have wandered into places they aren't supposed to be."

Max and Sophie glanced around and took a step towards each other.

"And don't ask what it does when it finds them," I said. "You don't want to know."

"Why? What does it do?" Max asked.

"It wraps them in its long, ghostly tendrils..."

"Yes?"

"It carries them to its lair, deep within the castle walls..."

Sophie let out a whimper. Max took a shaky breath. "And?"

LAIR THIS WAY

"And then … it drinks their blood!"

Max blinked. "It what?"

"It drinks their blood!" I said, waving my hands in the air for effect.

"Ghosts don't drink blood. Vampires drink blood," Max snorted. "You're making it up."

He glanced at his sister, who was shaking from head to toe, and looked like she might burst into tears at any moment.

"Well, Sophie believes me," I pointed out.

"She'll believe anything," Max said with a shrug, "but you can't fool me. I'm not scared of no Piddington Phantom."

The moment the words left Max's lips, there was a bang from outside the room that made us all jump. Slowly, surely, the door began to creak open, inch by ominous inch.

Sophie whimpered.

Max gasped.

And a tall grey shape appeared in the doorway.

CHAPTER 4

LEAVING THE CASTLE

For someone who claimed not to believe in the Piddington Phantom, Max did a pretty convincing impression of someone who did.

"Die, phantom, die!" he screamed, swinging wildly with what was probably a very expensive antique sword. Like I said, he's a heavy kid, but the sword was clearly much heavier. As he attempted to hack the grey figure into tiny bits, he was thrown off balance and sent staggering towards the door.

"Oi!" barked a castle guide, catching Max by the shoulders and putting a stop to his spinning. "What're you lot doing in here?"

Sophie grabbed my sleeve. "Is that the ghost?" she whispered.

"No, of course it isn't, silly," I said, trying to sound as reassuring as I could. "He just works for the ghost and does its evil bidding."

"You lot shouldn't be in here," the guide said. There was something about the way he wore his uniform – buttons shiny, trousers immaculately pressed – that gave me the impression he took his job very seriously. We were on the brink of getting into some pretty big trouble. Luckily, I had a strategy all worked out.

"We're castle inspectors," I told him. "From the Ministry of Castles and Stately Homes."

"You what?"

I put an ear to the closest wall, tapped one of the stone blocks and shook my head sadly.

"And I have to say, we're very disappointed with what we've found here today."

The guide tutted. "Think I was born yesterday, do you? You're just a bunch of kids who've wandered into somewhere you're not supposed to be."

Catching one of Max's arms the man took a step towards me and Sophie, his other hand making a grab for us. Sophie screamed and ducked behind me. "Don't let him take me to the ghost!"

"What ghost?" demanded the guide. "What're you on about?"

Sophie screamed again. "Th-that ghost!"

Her arm reached past me, finger outstretched. We all looked round in time to see a large grey shape sail through the air above the length of red rope. Its eerie outline flapped and fluttered as it seemed to float towards us.

Then, with a bark, the shape landed on the ground. The grey tapestry it had been tangled in fell to the floor, revealing Destructo. He bounded over to me, jumping up excitedly and trying to lick my face.

"No dogs allowed!" the guide bellowed. "And what's it done to that tapestry?"

With the guide distracted, Max took the opportunity to kick him hard on the shin and pull his arm free.

"Ow! I'll get you for that, you little monster," said the guide, hopping and clutching at his leg.

Excited by all the noise, Destructo ran in circles, knocking the man off his feet and sending him crashing down on top of the fallen armour. The guide looked up from the floor in time to see the dog lifting his leg and peeing happily on another tapestry hanging from one of the walls.

"Well, *clearly* this dog is not supposed to be here," I said, grabbing Destructo by the collar and dragging him towards the door. "We'll take it outside and find its rightful owner before it causes any more damage."

"Get back here!" the guide growled. "Don't you run off!"

Running off was exactly what I had in mind. Sophie, Max and I ducked under the rope, with me pulling Destructo along behind. Once we were out of the room, Destructo ran ahead, almost tearing my arm off. I let him go and we raced after him along the corridors, hunting for the rest of the family.

"Ghost! There's a ghost!" cried Sophie as we dodged through a throng of tourists. They looked at us in surprise, then flattened themselves against the wall in fright at the sight of the enormous grey hound racing along in front of us.

Mum, Dad, Jodie, Jas and Steve all turned as we hurried towards them.

"How did the dog get in here?" asked Mum.

"Destructo, sit!" said Jodie. Destructo sat down,  mid-run, and slid the last few metres on his bottom. "How did the dog get in here?" she demanded.

Jas looked down at Sophie. "Did you say 'ghost'?"

"Hmm? No," I said, skidding to a stop on the slippery stone floor. "She said, um, 'gas'. There's a gas leak. We have to leave."

"No, she didn't!" Max protested. "She said gho—"

I clamped my hand over Max's mouth. He might have a knack for avoiding trouble, but the same couldn't be said for me. If he told Mum and Dad about the chaos we'd caused, I'd be grounded for a week.

I glanced back to make sure the guide hadn't

tracked us down yet. "Ssh now, Max. Remember, they told us not to make a fuss so we don't cause mass panic. The last thing they want is everyone stampeding for the exit at the same time. It'd be chaos!"

We looked around at the empty corridor. The half-dozen tourists who had been gazing blankly at the grey walls had now filed out quietly. "Well, maybe 'chaos' is a strong word," I admitted. "But someone might fall over or lightly graze their elbow or something, and they just can't take that chance."

Somewhere, not too far away,  I heard the angry voice of the guide. I smiled, probably a little too broadly. "Everyone ready, then?"

"It cost three quid each for us to get in," Dad pointed out. He's a real skinflint. Even when he's having a completely terrible time, he'll stick something out until the bitter end so he gets maximum value for money.

"I'd happily pay twice that to get back out," Jas said.

I took hold of Destructo's collar and started to lead us to the exit.

Jodie yanked her earphone out of her ear. "What's happening now?" she asked.

"There's a gas leak,"  I said. "We have to leave."

"A gas leak? How could there be a gas leak?" yelled Jodie. "It's a fifteenth-century castle – they didn't have gas."

I peeked round a corner to make sure the guide wasn't lurking nearby. The coast was clear.

"Well, they do now," I said. "Too much of it, if anything. That's why it's leaking."

We turned the corner and made our way down a flight of steps and towards the open front door.

"Come on, keep up," I urged, glancing back up the stairs in case we were being followed. "We don't want to get gas poisoning."

"What I don't understand," muttered Dad, who

was dawdling at the back of the group, "is how on earth Destructo got out of the car."

We all stood in the car park, staring at Aunt Jas and Steve's car. It was a nice car. Or, at least, it had been.

"That'll probably just tape back on," I said, bending to pick up the rear windscreen which lay on the ground, completely intact.

Destructo sat beside the back bumper, his tail wagging as he gazed proudly at his handiwork.

"It pushed the window out," Jas muttered. "That ... beast pushed the back window out."

"Could've been worse," I said. "At least he hasn't chewed any of the seats to bits!"

I peered in through the gap where the window had been. There was white foam stuffing over every surface. "Oh no, I tell a lie. He has."

Jas threw her arms up in frustration. "Brilliant! Well, isn't that just great?"

"Come on, cutie-smoosh, it's not that bad," said Steve, but Jas quickly cut him dead.

"Not that bad, Steve? *Not that bad?* Look at it! That dog's trashed the windscreen and ripped up half the seats."

Steve held his hands up to try to calm her down. "I'm just saying, it's not really the dog's fault."

"How is it not the dog's fault?" Jas snapped. "Whose fault is it, then? Hmm, Steve? Did you destroy the car? Did I?"

Mum stepped between them. "It's OK. Calm down. We'll pay for it."

Dad's ears pricked up. "Eh?! I mean... I'm sure their insurance will cover it."

Jas turned on him. "No, actually, I don't think the insurance covers the car being eaten by an enormous dog."

"Partially eaten," I corrected, then shifted uncomfortably as Jas shot me a furious glare.

There was lots of muttering after that. Aunt Jas got in the driver's seat and slammed the door behind her. Destructo bounded back into the boot through the missing window, and everyone else squashed into their seats.

"Well, what a brilliant day this is turning out to be," Jodie mumbled, digging an elbow into my ribs.

"Statistically, it can only get better," I said.

Little did we know, though, it was actually about to get much, much worse.

CHAPTER 5

DRIVING HOME

"How come I've got the chewed-up one?" Jodie demanded, wriggling uncomfortably on the ruined remains of the seat.

I winced as if in pain, gingerly rubbing the base of my spine. "My bad back. I couldn't possibly sit on that," I said, fighting back a grin. "Also, it's probably a bit of a deathtrap, what with the seatbelt fastener having been gnawed to pieces. Plus, Mum and Dad love me more, so that's why you've got that seat."

"We do not love you more," Mum called from

the seats in front. She had to shout quite loudly to make herself heard over the roaring wind coming through the gaping hole where the rear windscreen should have been. Steve had wedged the windscreen into the boot, standing on its end, in the hope it would stop Destructo jumping out. There's no way it would stop him if he wanted to get out, but we were going pretty fast and even Destructo wasn't that dumb.

I gasped. "You mean ... you love *her* more? Impossible! Anyway, didn't you say you found her in a skip, and she's not really even part of the family?"

Jodie thumped me on the leg. I bit my lip and forced a smile. "That totally didn't even hurt," I said, crying on the inside.

"No, we didn't say that and you know it." Dad sighed. He had Max sitting on his knee, and his expression suggested he'd quite like to chuck him out of the window.

I turned to Sophie, who was perched on my right, her wide eyes darting anxiously at the motorway whizzing by outside. "Hey. You're not still scared about that whole ghost thing, are you?"

She nodded. "A bit."

"Well, you shouldn't be," I said. "There's no point worrying about a silly ghost! I mean, yes, one day it'll find you. Maybe not today. Maybe not tomorrow. But some day it will find us all. And when it does..."

"Ignore him," said Jodie. "He's lying. As usual."

"Why would I lie about something like that?"

"Because you lie about everything," Jodie said. "You can't help it. It's like you've got an illness."

"You're the one who's got an illness," I told her.

Jodie shook her head. "Weak comeback."

"No, I mean it," I said. "Didn't Mum show you the letter from the hospital? They're not saying it's *definitely* fatal, just that it probably is."

66

"Hilarious," Jodie scowled.

I patted her hand. "Good to see you're putting such a brave face on it."

We sat in silence for a while, listening to the roaring of the road beneath the tyres, and the howling of the wind behind our heads. Up in front, Jas and Steve were arguing, but it was impossible to make out what they were saying.

Sophie looked up at me, her eyes wide. "Do you think my mum and dad are going to get divorced?" she asked, biting her lip.

"Of course not," I smiled. "They're not married, so technically they'll just separate."

Jodie dug an elbow into my ribs. "But that won't happen, either," I quickly added.

Sophie wiped her eyes on her sleeve. "Are you sure?"

"Trust me," I said. "Everything's going to be totally fine."

Just then, the car swung violently left, throwing us all to the right. Sophie screamed. Max laughed.

With her seatbelt gone, Jodie had to brace herself against the seat in front to stop herself sprawling on to the floor.

With a screeching of brakes the car skidded to a stop. I thought we must have hit something, but then Jas yanked on the handbrake and turned angrily to Steve.

"I'm not an idiot, Steve. I do know the way to my sister's house!"

Steve held up his hands. "I'm not saying you don't," he protested. "I was just reminding you that the turning was coming up."

"How did you know? Hmm?" fumed Aunt Jas. "Was there a big picture of a dragon showing the way?"

Mum and Dad shot each other a worried glance. Everyone else just sat in awkward silence, except Destructo, who lay in the back noisily licking his bottom with a breathtaking amount of enthusiasm.

"Still, no harm done, eh?" said Mum, cheerfully.

Jas held up an open palm, silencing her. "Stay out of this, Claire."

"I'm just trying to help," Mum said. Before Jas could reply, Dad leaned right over into the front and turned up the radio.

"This is one of mine," he said, without a hint of shame. "For a fly spray. Join in if you know the words!" He took a deep breath just as the jingle hit top gear.

"**You're *so* annoying, just leave me alone, you're driving me crazy, get out of my home,**" he sang, giving it lots of elbow action which made Max wobble around on Dad's knees. "**It's time to say bye-bye, I wish that you'd just die...**"

His voice trailed off when he realized everyone in the car was staring at him. Even Destructo had paused, mid-bottom lick, to look Dad's way.

Quietly, Dad cleared his throat. "Sorry," he said. "Those lyrics possibly weren't helping."

It all kicked off then. Jas started shouting at Steve. Mum started moaning at Dad. Destructo started barking his head off, while Sophie burst into tears and Max took great delight in punching the car roof over and over again.

Jodie scowled at me. "This is your fault."

"How is this my fault?" I asked.

"Because of all your lies. They caused this!"

I shook my head. "I find that very hard to believe," I said. Jodie tutted then turned away.

We had pulled off the main road into an industrial estate. A few people walked past the car, shooting us sideways glances. I was tempted to hold up a sign telling them I'd been kidnapped, but instead just smiled broadly and gave them a wave as they hurried by.

Eventually, as the din reached fever pitch, Mum turned to Jodie and me. "Look," she said,

"why don't you two go and find a takeaway and pick us all up some fish and chips for lunch? Me and your dad will take Max and Sophie to a park to give Aunt Jas and Steve a chance to work things out."

"A park?" said Dad. "We're in the middle of an industrial estate. Where are we going to find a park?"

"We'll find one," said Mum, very deliberately. "How difficult can it be? Here." She thrust a twenty-pound note into Jodie's hands, then slid open the side door and gestured for us all to pile out.

"We'll be back soon," Mum said to Jas, but she and Steve were so busy arguing they didn't even notice us getting out of the car.

As soon as he was set free, Max punched Dad in the groin with all his might, then ran off laughing. Dad hobbled after him, swearing below his breath, while Mum and Sophie hurried to catch up.

Jodie folded her arms and looked up and down the road. Factories, warehouses and rundown garages lined both sides of the street.

"Where are we meant to find a chip shop round here?" she sighed.

"Don't worry, I know where there's one," I announced. Picking a direction at random, I set off at a brisk pace which suggested I knew exactly where I was going. "Follow me, I'll get us there in no time!"

Jodie growled. "You have no idea where you're going, do you?"

"Please. I know exactly where I'm going," I said.

"No, you don't. We've passed that same shop four times in the past twenty minutes," Jodie said, pointing across the road to a second-hand furniture shop which I had to admit did look a bit familiar.

"All these little furniture places look the same."

"Do they all have the same name and the same

woman standing in the doorway?" Jodie asked. "Look, she's even waving at us she's seen us so often."

"She's not waving," I said. "She's … polishing a butterfly."

Jodie stopped. "Aaargh! Why do you always do this?"

"Do what?" I asked innocently.

Jodie shot me her "I'm about to hurt you" Look, which I knew only too well.

"Lie all the time!" she cried. "Like at the castle, there wasn't really a gas leak."

"There was—" I protested, but she cut me off.

"There was not. Why can't you tell the truth, Beaky? For once!"

Somehow, she had seen through my cunning ruse. OK, it wasn't all that cunning, but Jodie seemed pretty gullible most of the time. Either that or she couldn't be bothered calling me out on my lies. Recently, though, she'd questioned nearly everything I said. She clearly wasn't falling for the gas leak lie. That left only one option: tell a different one.

"You're right, there wasn't a gas leak," I admitted.

"Thank you."

"It was a radiation leak. The castle has got a nuclear reactor in the basement. I thought I'd better get Max and Sophie to safety before they mutated and turned green or something, and ruined everyone's weekend."

Jodie hit me with the full force of the Look. Any moment now she was going to hurt me, but how?

A Chinese burn?

A nipple twister?

A spinning roundhouse
kick to the head?

She'd done them all before. Although that last one might have been a dream, now I think about it.

In the end, she just shook her head and stormed off along the road. "Whatever."

I caught her up. "You believe me?"

"Of course I don't believe you!" she said, but then she stopped and looked over my shoulder. "Hey, what's that?"

I wasn't about to fall for that one. She'd snag me with a wedgie the second I turned round. This was amateur-level stuff and, frankly, I expected more of her.

I was halfway through telling her that when she pushed me aside and barged past.

We were standing outside a strange little shop that I was sure we hadn't passed before. It looked like the type of place you'd find decorating a biscuit tin at the back of your gran's cupboard – all twiddly writing and tiny windowpanes that had the appearance of rippling water.

"Madame Shirley's Marvellous Emporium of Peculiarities," said Jodie, reading the hand-painted sign.

The stuff in the window didn't look all that "peculiar" – more like a load of old junk. There was a tatty ragdoll in a rocking chair, a model of a frog playing a banjo and a saggy old stuffed toy cat with half its fur missing.

Beside those was a whole rack filled with nothing but pickled onion crisps. That was pretty peculiar, I suppose.

And beside that was a handwritten sign.

"Try the world's only truth-telling machine," Jodie read. "That's a bit weird."

I nodded. "A truth-telling machine. How ridiculous."

"No, I mean … we were just talking about how you're such a liar…"

"No, we weren't," I lied.

"…and now here's a shop advertising the world's only truth-telling machine."

"You don't really believe there's such a thing as a machine that makes people tell the truth, do you?" I asked. I sounded confident, but there was a tiny doubt niggling away at the back of my mind. Could there be such a machine? I snorted. *Nah.*

"Can't hurt to try, can it?" said Jodie. Her eyes lit up. She caught my arm. And before I could stop her, she dragged me through the door and into the strange little shop.

CHAPTER 6

THE TRUTH-TELLING MACHINE

The inside of the shop smelled of one part mould, one part cabbage, and eight parts pickled onion crisps. A little bell chimed above the door as we entered, and something that looked like a startled scarecrow popped up from behind the counter.

"Madame Shirley at your service!" roared the scarecrow. "A joy to meet you, an absolute joy!"

"Well, this is ... nice," I said, looking around at the clutter of dusty books, broken ornaments, tins of cat food and yet more bags of pickled onion crisps. It wasn't so much an *Emporium of Peculiarities* as it was a cramped, dimly-lit shop filled with mad old junk.

Madame Shirley was as much of a jumble as the shop was. Her greying hair stood on end like she'd spent the morning rubbing balloons on it, and her skinny frame was tucked inside either a very long dress or a very small tent. She wore purple fingerless gloves and had three pairs of glasses on strings round her neck.

As she made her way round the shop counter, she knocked a stack of old magazines, a small wooden clock and a tub of margarine on to the floor. She stepped over the pile and rushed to meet us.

"Come in, come in," she cackled, apparently oblivious to the fact that we already were in. "Come for a browse, have you? Come for a nosey?"

"Actually, we've come for the truth-telling machine," Jodie said, indicating the sign in the window.

"Don't listen to her," I said. "We're here for crisps. I don't suppose you have any...?"

Madame Shirley squinted and looked me up and down. "Yes. Oh my, yes, I see why you're here. And just in time, too," she muttered. She held her hand out to Jodie, still staring at me with her beady little eyes. "Pound."

Jodie hesitated, then fished in her pocket and handed over a pound coin. Madame Shirley bit it, nodded once, then caught my arm and guided me through a maze of teetering boxes towards the back of the shop.

"What's with all the pickled onion crisps?" I asked.

Madame Shirley rolled her eyes. "There was a mistake with the order. It's absolutely ridiculous, isn't it? I mean, why on earth would anyone need so many packets of pickled onion crisps?" she said,

shaking her head. "They were supposed to be salt and vinegar."

"Riiiight," I said slowly. "That would make *much* more sense."

We stopped in a shadowy corner of the shop.

"Now," breathed Madame Shirley. "Here we are."

I don't know what I expected to see. A small but exciting fairground ride, maybe. A colourful doorway with some glitter on it, perhaps. Even just a shower cubicle with some Christmas lights dangling off it would have done.

Madame Shirley's machine, though, was none of these things.

A large dented metal box stood in the corner of the shop. It reminded me of the portaloos we had to use at school when the pipes all froze a few years ago. On the door, someone had scribbled "truth-telling machine" in blue felt-tip pen.

I turned to Jodie and grinned. "Well, this all seems completely genuine."

"OK, yes. Daft idea," she admitted.

"Nonsense! We haven't come from all the way *just out there on the street* to turn back now," I gloated. "I'm sure this rusty box will teach me a very valuable lesson indeed."

Madame Shirley muttered below her breath as she tugged and heaved on the door. "Come on, you ruddy thing." She gave it a kick, before eventually managing to open it with a squeal of rusty metal.

"Now that's proper craftsmanship, that is," I said admiringly.

Jodie scowled and crossed her arms. She was clearly feeling stupid for believing the sign in the window. I knew the decent thing to do would be to leave the shop, pretend none of it had happened and let her off the hook.

No chance! I was going to milk this for all it was worth.

I stepped into the
box and a lightbulb
flickered on above
my head. The metal
walls were bare and
featureless. Other than
me and the bulb, the box
was completely empty.

The door squeaked shut.

"They don't make 'em like this any more,"
I said, my voice bouncing around inside the narrow
chamber.

I whistled quietly, listening to the echo and
waiting for the door to open. I imagined how much
Jodie would be cringing with embarrassment right
now. I'd never let her live this down. I couldn't wait
to tell all her friends that she'd fallen for—

The floor began to vibrate gently.

I looked down.

"Huh," I said.

A second later, the world turned inside out.

Imagine being inside a washing machine on high spin. Now imagine that washing machine is tumbling down a hill. During an earthquake. On the moon. That's not even close to what it was like inside the truth-telling machine. Part of me knew I wasn't actually moving, but the rest of me felt like I was being flipped and twirled and shaken and spun in every direction at once.

I could see my feet were still standing on the floor, but the floor became the ceiling and the walls became the door and the whole thing kept flipping end over end. I looked at my hands, which suddenly seemed a very long way away, and somehow got the impression they were looking back at me.

My head spun. My stomach heaved. My eyes rolled like the barrels of a fruit machine. I tried to speak, but my throat was dry, my lungs had cramped up, and the sound was point-blank refusing to come out.

And then, without any warning, the whole thing shuddered to a stop.

I leaned my hand against the door to steady myself, then almost fell flat on my face when Madame Shirley pulled it open.

I stumbled out, trying hard to A) stay upright, and B) not vomit. Jodie and Madame Shirley looked at me with very different expressions.

"Well?" asked Madame Shirley, beaming from ear to ear. "How was it?"

"What do you mean, 'how was it'?" said Jodie. "Nothing happened! He just went in the box, hung about for five seconds and came back out again."

Five seconds? Was that all I'd been in there for? It felt like much longer.

The machine may have stopped spinning, flipping and shaking, but my brain hadn't. I had no idea what had gone on in there, but if Jodie saw what a dizzy mess I was, it would be her who would never let *me* live it down. I swallowed and tried to pull myself together.

Play it cool, Beaky. Play it cool. Don't let them see how shaken up you are.

I shrugged. I smiled.

"I did a little wee," I announced.

Wait.

Back up.

What?

Jodie snorted. "Sorry?"

My head was obviously more scrambled than I thought. I took a breath and tried again.

"I did a little wee," I said, pointing to the front of my trousers. "In my pants."

With a gasp, I clamped my hand over my mouth. Why had I said that? I mean, it was true, but why had I said it?

I looked at Madame Shirley. She winked one of her beady little eyes and gave me a fingerless-glove thumbs up. "Another satisfied customer," she laughed.

"What…? But … I mean… What have you done to me?" I demanded.

The old lady looked at the truth-telling machine then waggled her bushy eyebrows. I shook my head, refusing to believe it. It couldn't be true. The stupid machine was just a rusty old box. It couldn't actually have worked.

Could it?

Frantically, I tried a lie. Something simple would be enough. I'd say how much I'd enjoyed being in the machine. Nice and easy.

"That was *horrible*," I said, letting out a loud sob. "It was all spinning and flipping and I thought I was going to die."

OK. So maybe not *that* easy.

I tried again.

"Your shoes are white," I said to Jodie. Then I smacked myself on the forehead and jumped up and down in frustration. "Aaargh! No!"

88

Jodie raised an eyebrow and looked down at her trainers. "Yeah. So?"

"I was trying to say they were orange," I cried. "But somewhere between here–" I tapped myself on the side of the head – "and here–" I pointed to my mouth – "orange became white. And I don't know why!"

I grabbed Madame Shirley by the shoulders. "What's happening? Make it stop!"

Madame Shirley smiled. "Oh, no, I can't do that. It's a one-way street, you see. I couldn't very well have a machine that made people lie all the time, could I? That'd be skating on some very thin ice, that would. Moral-wise."

She smiled, then held out a small green bag. "Crisp?"

"Wait, so … what's happening, exactly?" Jodie frowned.

"It's her," I said, stepping back and pointing at Madame Shirley. She smirked and continued munching on her crisps. "She's a woman!"

Jodie blinked. "Er, yes. And?"

"No, not a woman! I don't mean she's a woman," I said. "I mean she's a *woman*!"

"OK, then," said Jodie brightly. "That makes things much clearer."

"I suspect what he's trying to say is that I'm a witch," said Madame Shirley, licking the pickled-onion flavouring from the tips of her fingers. "But deep down he knows I'm not, so he can't get the words out."

Jodie looked at me. She looked at Madame Shirley. After a few seconds, she gave a nod. "Right. OK. I get it," she said, shooting me a scowl. "You're winding me up. Very funny. You want me to believe the machine worked."

"It did work," I protested.

"You should listen to him," said Madame Shirley. "He's telling the truth. No choice in the matter now, have you, lad?"

Jodie tutted and made for the door. "Fine. Whatever. Ha ha, the joke's on me."

"Jodie, wait," I said, hurrying after her. She stormed past the shelves of junk and racks of crisps and out on to the street.

"Cheerio!" called Madame Shirley. "Pleasure doing business with you. Please come again!"

I spun on the spot. "I'll be right back," I said to her. "Then we're going to fix me."

The old lady just smiled.

I darted out of the shop. "Jodie, wait. Come back," I said.

With a sigh, Jodie stopped and turned round. "What?" she demanded.

"OK, OK, listen," I began. "I know this sounds crazy, but that machine…"

"Metal box," Jodie corrected.

"Whatever it was … it worked," I said. "I can't lie."

"Well, you're lying now, obviously," Jodie said, turning to go.

I caught her by the arm. "Wait, no, don't go," I pleaded. "We have to go back in the shop and…"

I looked at the door just in time to see Madame Shirley turn the lock on the inside and pull down a blind.

"No, no, no!" I groaned, racing back and rapping my knuckles on the glass. "What are you doing? Open the door."

The blind came back up and I breathed a sigh of relief. Madame Shirley gave me a friendly wave, then turned her little "Open" sign so it read "Closed". With a *swish* she pulled the blind back down again.

I thumped my fist against the door. "Open up! Open up! You can't leave me like this!"

"Beaky, what are you doing?" Jodie asked. She sounded annoyed, but I could pretty much guarantee she wasn't as annoyed as I was.

I bent down and flipped open the shop's letterbox. "Open up or I'll try to kick the door down, but probably fail miserably because of my poor lower body strength," I shouted through  the gap. "Pretend you didn't hear that last bit," I added, after a pause.

"The joke's over," said Jodie. "Come on, we need to get those fish and chips."

"You don't believe me," I muttered, my mind racing. "Of course you don't believe me, because I lie all the time, like the time I said I didn't know what happened to your goldfish. Or all those times I used your toothbrush to clean my bike and told you I hadn't."

"I *knew* it," Jodie cried. She crossed her arms. "But I still don't believe you on the 'not being able to lie' thing."

"Fine," I said, squaring my shoulders. "Well, if you don't believe me, then I guess there's nothing else for it. I'm just going to have to prove it."

CHAPTER 7

THE JOURNEY HOME

Jodie power-walked along the street, keeping a look-out for anything resembling a chip shop. I hurried to keep up, glancing back to see if Madame Shirley had come out of her shop, just before we rounded a corner and I lost sight of the place.

"Go on, then," I urged. "Ask me anything."

Jodie shook her head. "You're just not going to give up, are you? Fine. What happened to my goldfish?"

"Destructo knocked the bowl over. I tried to catch it. The fish went out the window," I said.

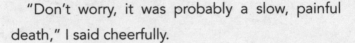

"I didn't see what happened to it after that, but as it fell five metres on to solid concrete, I'm assuming it was nothing good."

"I knew it was you!" Jodie gasped. She shook her head. "Poor Sharky. I loved that fish."

"Don't worry, it was probably a slow, painful death," I said cheerfully.

Jodie's jaw dropped. "Oh, well, that's made me feel much better."

I clenched my fists and beat them against the sides of my head. "Argh! That's not what I meant to say."

Jodie stopped and eyed me suspiciously. "How often do you change your pants?"

"Three times a week at most," I said.

"Socks?"

"Twice a week. But sometimes I just turn them inside out."

She tapped her foot. Her eyes narrowed. She held out a hand. "Give me your phone."

"What? Why?"

Jodie scowled. "Do you want me to believe you or not?"

Reluctantly, I handed her my mobile. I knew she couldn't do too much harm with the screen locked.

"What's your security code?" Jodie asked.

"I'm not telling you that!" I said.

She held out the phone to me. "See? I knew you were lying."

I stared at the handset, then at my sister's smug expression. I didn't want to tell her, but if it proved I was telling the truth, it might be worth it. Besides, I could feel the numbers rising up in my throat, like they were determined to come out all on their own.

"Four-nine-two-one," I said through gritted teeth.

Jodie punched in the PIN and the screen unlocked. I made a grab for the phone, but she held me at arm's length with one hand.

"OK, give it back, I proved it," I said.

Jodie tapped the screen a few times with her thumb. "Do you have any embarrassing selfies on here?"

I bit my lip. "Yes, loads."

"Good to know!" Jodie grinned.

I tried another grab for the mobile, but she ducked out of the way. "Oooh yes, here's one."

"Give it back!" I demanded.

Jodie's thumb flew across the screen. "Just emailing this to myself, and ... done."

She held the phone out and I snatched it back straight away. I groaned when I saw the picture on screen. It was taken from a low angle and you could see right up my nostrils. To be fair, from that view my nose did look pretty massive.

"What are you going to do with that photo?" I asked.

Jodie shrugged. "Anything I want. Facebook. Instagram. I'll put it *everywhere*," she said, smiling wickedly. "Unless you admit you're lying about the truth-telling thing."

My heart raced. What to do? If that picture got out I'd be a laughing stock. There was no way Jodie was going to believe me, so if I wanted to stop her posting my big-nosed selfie everywhere, there was only one thing for it – I had to tell a lie.

I could do this. I hadn't lost the knack, this was just a temporary glitch, and with enough concentration and willpower, I could force out a fib. If I didn't, that terrible selfie would go viral in a matter of minutes.

I flexed my fingers and took a series of deep breaths. Yes, I could do this. I could do it!

"All the stuff about the truth-telling machine," I began.

Jodie leaned in. "Yes?"

"It was a I..."

"A what?"

"A I... A I..." The word was stuck in my mouth and wouldn't come out. I could almost feel it wedged in there, somewhere behind my teeth. I threw up my hands in despair. There was no point fighting it. "I can't do it. It was the truth, OK? The machine really did work."

Jodie held up her phone. "Instagram, Beaky. Remember? I'll tag everyone. *Everyone*. Is that what you really want?"

I slumped down on to the step of a shop. "Fine. Do it. I can't stop you."

A shadow passed over me. I looked up to see

Jodie staring down. Her eyebrows met as she frowned. "Are you being serious?"

"Yes. I am. Something weird happened in that box. Everything went all sort of … swooshy, and now I can't tell a lie," I said. "Also, the step is making my bum cold."

"Too much information," Jodie said. She kept looking at me for a few moments, deep in thought. Then she held out a hand. "Come on. Let's go back to the shop and find out what's going on."

We walked for ten minutes, marching down alleys and side streets, retracing our steps over and over again. But no matter how hard we looked, we couldn't find Madame Shirley's shop anywhere.

"Where is it?" I yelped, pulling at my hair as I spun on the spot. "It was around here somewhere. It can't have just vanished!"

"I don't know," Jodie said, glancing at her watch.

"But we've been gone for ages. Mum and Dad are going to kill us. We have to get back."

"What? No, we can't. We have to fix me!"

"I'm sorry, Beaky. We've tried, but we have to get back. But look on the bright side," Jodie said. "You can't lie any more, which means you're less likely to get into trouble, and I'm less likely to beat you up. Maybe this is an improvement."

I shook my head. "Not for me, it isn't!"

Jodie made a weighing motion with her hands. "You. Everyone else in the world." One hand dropped lower. "Oh, look. Everyone else in the world wins. Now come on, let's find some fish and chips and get back to the car."

"But..."

"Instagram, Beaky," Jodie warned. "Don't make me say it again!"

Jodie was right, Mum and Dad were pretty unimpressed about how long we'd been gone, in spite of us having tracked down the only fish and chip shop for miles. I knew the situation with Jas and Steve hadn't improved, because Mum wasn't even bothering to be cheerful now.

Normally in situations like these she'd try to jolly everyone along, but she was just sitting in her seat, angrily stuffing chips into her mouth. Dad kept

muttering about Max's behaviour at the park, while crunching noisily on crispy bits of fish batter.

Max, meanwhile, was sitting on the chewed-up seat and shouting at the top of his voice as he

violently rocked back and forth. Sophie watched him in her usual eerie silence.

Up front, Jas and Steve were staring pointedly in opposite directions, eating their fish and chips in silence.

"Well, looks like our journey home's going to be unpleasant for everyone," I announced, clambering into the car. Jodie had managed to make it in ahead of me, and was now sitting in my seat, between Max and Sophie.

"I was sitting there," I said.

"And now you aren't," said Jodie.

I looked to Mum and Dad for help, but they weren't volunteering any. "Mum, Dad, can Max sit up there with—"

"No!" they replied in unison.

I glanced around the car. "Well, where am I supposed to sit?"

Destructo's head appeared over the back of the rear seats. He panted happily, dribbling drool over the upholstery.

I sighed. "You have got to be kidding me."

I tried to claim a bad back, but instead confessed that I'd been lying about that the whole time, which earned a loud cry of triumph from Jodie and a "We'll talk about this later" from Dad.

For the rest of the journey home I sat squashed in the boot, sharing my now almost cold fish and chips with Destructo. Although, when I say

"sharing" I mean that he ate most of it when I wasn't looking, then spent the rest of the car ride chewing the box.

Over on the other side of the back seats, Max let out a yelp of disgust. "Ugh, what's that smell?"

"That was me," I confessed. "Fish makes me fart."

"Dylan!" Mum snapped.

"Well, it's true," I said.

"That may be, but nobody wants to hear it."

"There'll be another one brewing in a minute," I said.

NEARLY DONE

"Dylan! Cut it out."

"Didn't you know? That's his new thing now," I heard Jodie say. "He tells the truth all the time. It's hilarious."

Jodie may have found it funny then, but I had a feeling she wouldn't be laughing for long…

CHAPTER 8

A NOVEL ARGUMENT

When we got home, I waited for everyone to use the bathroom, then I hurried inside and locked the door. I spent the next few hours staring into the mirror and giving myself a motivational pep talk.

"Lying is easy, Beaky," I said. "You're an Olympic-level liar. You could lie in your sleep, you big liar, you!"

I then spent another hour holding up a toothbrush and trying to say it was a giraffe. I didn't have much success. It was a toothbrush and I knew it, which meant calling it anything else would be a lie, and even after all my motivational speeches, lying was still proving impossible. The closest I got was "gtoothbrush", and even that was more by accident than anything else.

I took out my phone and sent Theo a text:

`Something has happened. I can't lie any more.`

I sat on the closed toilet lid, waiting for his reply. Theo was a practical sort of guy. He'd have some ideas as to what I could do.

The phone buzzed. I tapped the screen.

`Liar :)` said the reply.

I tapped the keyboard. `It's true`, I wrote, then tried to prove it by adding, `I fancy Miss Gavistock from the school canteen`.

I waited for the reply, but before it came there was a soft knock on the door. "Dylan, love?" said Aunt Jas. "Are you on the loo?"

"No. I can't comfortably poo with so many people in the house," I admitted.

Jas hesitated. "OK. Well, that's … enlightening,

thanks. It's just that you've been in there for hours and Sophie needs to go."

I stood up. "Just coming," I said.

My phone buzzed and I hurriedly tapped the screen, hoping to find some words of wisdom from Theo. Instead, all he'd written was one word: Weirdo.

With a sigh, I put the phone in my pocket and made for the door. Before I left, though, I grabbed the toothbrush and held it up to my reflection. "Toothbrush!" I declared, then I sighed and tossed the brush back in the cup. I couldn't even lie by surprise.

When I opened the door, Sophie was lurking right outside, which almost made me jump out of my skin.

"You're a very creepy child," I said, sidling past her.

She sidestepped into the bathroom and kept watching me until the door closed between us.

Back in the living room, the atmosphere was lighter than I'd expected. Mum and Dad were sitting at the table, drinking tea as they read the newspapers. Steve was on one of the sofas with Max sprawled on his lap, playing games on Steve's phone. Aunt Jas sat down beside Steve and for the briefest of brief moments they smiled at one another. It was over in a fraction of a second, but it was the first smile I'd seen pass between them since they'd arrived. Maybe everything was going to be OK, after all.

Jodie was curled up on Dad's armchair flicking through Facebook or Instagram or whatever, which left me an entire sofa to myself! I flopped down, then nearly jumped out of my skin for a second time as Sophie appeared beside me. One minute she wasn't there, the next she was.

"Wah! Where did you come from?" I gasped.

A full minute seemed to pass before Sophie answered. "Bathroom."

"Did you teleport?" I asked.

Another lengthy pause, then, "Nope."

I nodded. "Right, then. Good. Good." I turned to the rest of the family. "So, how is everyone?" I asked, far too enthusiastically.

"Very well, thank you, Dylan," said Mum. "You?"

"Oh, you know," I began. "Absolutely terrible."

"Is it because of the castle?" asked Jas. "It was a bit rubbish."

I shook my head. "No, no. Not the castle," I said. My voice was sounding increasingly high-pitched. I tried to bring it under control, but instead I just made it sound even more desperate. Words tumbled out of me and I got the feeling that even if I'd wanted to stop them, I couldn't.

"A weird woman with too many pickled onion crisps put me in a magic box that turned me inside out and did something to my brain," I explained. "And then she made her shop disappear when no one was looking."

Everyone stared. Then, a moment later, they all started to laugh … except for Sophie, who just kept on staring.

"Oh, Dylan," said Mum. "What an imagination."

"Brilliant," said Dad, leaping up from his chair. "Let me get my notebook. I might use that."

Dad reached under the coffee table and pulled out his notebook. He flipped to the back page and scribbled frantically.

"What's that, Dan?" Steve asked.

Dad held up the notebook proudly. "This little thing? It's just my novel."

"Ooooh," said Jas. "Check you out, Mr Writer."

"It's not finished," Dad said.

"I think they probably figured that out," I said. "Not many novels come handwritten."

Dad ignored me and instead looked at the notebook clutched in his hands. "Would you...? No," he said, waving a hand dismissively.

"Would we what?" Jas asked.

"Nothing, nothing," said Dad bashfully. "I was just going to ask if you wanted to hear some of it, that's all."

"Well, *duh*. Yes!" cried Jas.

"Absolutely not," I said, but once again everyone ignored me. Not only could I no longer lie, it seemed I had apparently turned invisible. Or inaudible. Or something.

Dad cleared his throat and flipped to the front of the notebook. He had been working on the book for months. Years, even. He'd told me the plot about six times now and each time it was completely different. This was the first time we were going to hear any of it read out loud, though. Maybe I was being too hard on him. Maybe he'd surprise me and the book would be brilliant.

"It was a dark and stormy night," he began.

Nope. It was going to be rubbish.

"That's a terrible opening," I said.

Dad peered at me over the top of the notebook.

"No, it isn't," he said. "It's … what do you call it…?"

"Atmospheric," said Mum.

"Exactly. Thank you, dear. It's atmospheric," Dad said. "It's setting the tone. Now, if you don't mind?"

He cleared his throat again, shot me a look that suggested I should probably keep my mouth shut, then began once more.

"It was a dark and stormy night…"

It wasn't easy to follow the story, but I'm not convinced there was even a story to follow, just a lot of sentences one after the other with the occasional pause for dramatic effect. Dad droned on.

And on.

And on.

As he was reading, I glanced around at everyone else. Aside from Max, who was fixated on whatever game he was playing, and Jodie, who was fixated on Facebook, everyone looked completely enthralled by Dad's reading.

What was wrong with these people? Even Destructo lay down and seemed to be listening in, although he may also have been asleep. It was hard to tell.

After a full hour, Dad lowered the notebook and smiled. "That's a taster. I could go on."

"God, don't!" I yelped.

Mum shot me a stern look as the others began to applaud. "Give your father a clap," she said.

With a sigh, I raised my hands. I tried to applaud, but some invisible force stopped my palms meeting at the very last moment. Mum raised the severity of her glare from "stern" to "angry" and I felt myself begin to sweat under the pressure.

STERN   ANGRY

Saying I enjoyed Dad's novel would be untrue, and applauding him for it would be just as much of a lie. If I didn't, though, Mum's glare would move up from "angry" to "grounded for a week".

I had an idea. Frantically, I looked my dad up and down. There had to be something about him worthy of applause. His hair was thinning at the top. He was a bit flabby round the belly and his clothes went out of fashion in the early nineties. Nothing to congratulate him on there.

His trainers! He had the whitest  trainers of anyone I knew. They almost glowed, and I'd always been amazed by how clean he managed to keep them. I focused on the trainers and forced my hands together. This time, they touched! Relieved, I clapped enthusiastically, which made Mum give me a nod and downgrade her glare. *Phew*. That was a close call. Luckily, I'd been able to pull the wool over everyone's eyes and...

Wait.

Oh, no.

The words came out all on their own. I tried to stop them, but there was nothing that could be done.

"I'm clapping for his trainers," I announced in a loud voice. "Not the novel, because that was terrible. He has very white trainers, though, and that's the only reason I'm clapping."

"Dylan!" Mum barked, and the other applause spluttered and died away.

A few seconds later, I realized I was still clapping. I stopped and clasped my hands in front of me.

"Anyone for tea?" I asked.

"Apologize to your father, Dylan," Mum said.

"No, no, wait," said Dad, holding up a hand. "I'd like to hear Dylan's thoughts."

I shook my head quickly. "No, you wouldn't."

"Yes, I would."

"Trust me, you definitely wouldn't."

Dad smiled. "I can take a bit of criticism, Dylan. Don't worry. Go for it."

"OK. You asked for it," I said. I took a deep breath, then launched into a detailed review of Dad's book.

I tore apart the flimsy characters, the boring writing, the non-existent plot. I ripped into his mixed metaphors, his rambling sentences, and the fact that none of the story – not one thing – made the tiniest bit of sense whatsoever.

"Oh," Dad said, but I wasn't finished.

"And you've got a really boring reading voice," I added, "which made the whole awful experience ten times worse. I even tried faking a nosebleed at one point, but that *stupid* machine wouldn't let me."

Slowly Dad sat down, his face an ashen grey. I looked around at the rest of the family. Everyone – even Max – was staring at me in disbelief. I smiled weakly. "Well, he did ask."

A well-timed "Just kidding!" here would have helped a lot, but as it would have been a lie, I couldn't come out with it. Instead, I frantically looked for a way to change the subject.

I jabbed a thumb in Sophie's direction. "Does she freak anyone else out, by the way?" I asked. "She reminds me of these twins I saw in a horror movie, once."

Mum stood up abruptly. "Right, Dylan, that's enough."

"Yeah, Beaky, cut it out," warned Jodie.

"Well, she does," I protested. "Dad agrees, don't you, Dad?"

Dad looked up from his notebook and shook his head. "What? No, I don't."

"Yes, you do! You said Sophie gave you the heebie-jeebies, and that Max was Satan in a pair of shorts."

120

"Cool!" said Max, grinning. He flicked a bogey at the TV screen as if to help Dad's case.

All eyes went to Dad, who shifted awkwardly. "I didn't say any of that. Dylan's making it up. Aren't you, Dylan?" he said, very deliberately.

I wanted to stop. More than anything, I wanted to stop. I knew every word I uttered was getting me deeper and deeper into trouble, but the truths were like a river flowing out of my mouth.

"No," I replied. "You almost choked to death when you found out Aunt Jas was coming, and Jodie said the kids should be in a zoo."

Jas's face went tight. "Oh, really? Is that true, Dan?"

Steve put a comforting hand on her leg, but Jas pushed it away, angrily.

"No, Steve, I want to hear what Dan's problem with me is."

"Dan doesn't have a problem with you," began Mum.

Jas scowled. "Shut up, Claire, I want to hear it from Dan."

"Don't you tell me to shut up," Mum replied, and before I knew it, everyone was on their feet, shouting at one another. Destructo got in on the act by barking loudly and running in circles, knocking over lamps and ornaments with his tail.

Jodie marched over to where I was sitting and grabbed me by the ear. "Garden. Now," she yelled, then she yanked me off the sofa with one painful tug.

Out in the garden, we could still hear the muffled sounds of everyone arguing inside. Jodie wagged an angry finger at me. "Joke's over, Beaky. Enough's enough. Go back to normal – or whatever passed for normal for you, at least."

"I keep telling you, I *can't*," I protested. Why couldn't she understand? "Do you think I'd be behaving like this on purpose? Do you think I want to be grounded for the rest of my life?"

"Yes," Jodie said. She deflated a little. "Maybe. I mean … I don't know."

"I'm not making it up. The machine really did work," I said, slumping down on to the back step and clutching my head in my hands. "Whoever Madame Shirley was, whatever her box did to me, I can't lie. And that's the truth."

"Then just keep your mouth shut," Jodie said, sighing. "Don't say anything and maybe we'll get through the weekend without—"

"I've tried that!" I yelped, leaping to my feet. "I didn't mean to say *any* of that stuff in there, but my lips wouldn't stop moving!"

"Well, then, go to bed or something," Jodie said. "But you're sleeping on the floor tonight," she added quickly.

She put her hand on the door handle and took a deep breath. Silence had fallen in the house. Who knew what awaited us inside?

"Here goes," Jodie said, and she opened the door.

When we returned to the living room, Aunt Jas and her family were nowhere to be seen. Dad was sitting at the dining table, scoring through the pages of his notebook with a  red pen. Mum, meanwhile, was fluffing up the sofa cushions with a level of violence usually reserved for professional boxing matches.

"Where is everyone?" Jodie asked.

"Bed," said Mum, not looking at us.

"It's barely nine o'clock," I said, but Mum just shot me a glare. "I mean … I think I'll go to bed now, too."

"You're not in Jodie's room tonight," said Mum, her voice clipped and hard. "You're back in your own room."

"That's great!" I said, more cheerfully than was probably good for me.

"With Steve, Sophie and Max," Mum added.

I felt my face fall. "What?"

"Jas is going in with Jodie tonight, so you're with Steve and your cousins."

I opened my mouth to reply, but Jodie dug an elbow into my ribs. "Goodnight, Beaky," she said, in a voice that was almost a growl.

I looked at Jodie. I looked at Mum. I looked at the door leading out into the hall. There was no point fighting it.

"Goodnight, everyone," I mumbled, and I trudged towards the door. Before I could reach it though, Mum stopped me.

"What were you thinking, Dylan?" she snapped. "Saying all that horrible stuff about everyone?"

"I couldn't help it," I said. "Besides, it's not like everyone else hasn't said it before, is it?"

"But not to their faces!" Dad said in a loud whisper.

I frowned. "How is that better?" I asked.

The room fell silent. Mum and Dad exchanged a glance, then shifted uncomfortably.

"Go to bed, Dylan," said Mum, and I was relieved to do just that.

CHAPTER 9

THE PAPERBOY

The good news was that I didn't have to sleep on the floor. The bad news was, I barely slept at all.

For the first few hours I lay on my top bunk, listening to Max playing on Steve's phone and talking non-stop about the many ways to die in whatever game he was playing.

Eventually they all fell asleep, and the bleeping was replaced by the sounds of Steve rolling about and muttering in his sleep in the bunk below. He's not the chattiest guy in the world when he's awake, but when he's sleeping he doesn't shut up!

Max and Sophie were in sleeping bags on the floor, and Max spent the night farting. Seriously, I was sure the room was slowly filling up with a green haze as he trumped and parped the whole night through.

At one point I looked over the side of the bed and saw Sophie lying on her back, staring up at me. At first, I thought she was wide awake, but soon realized she was sleeping with her eyes open, like some sort of demon vampire child.

Add to the muttering, wind-breaking and creepy staring the fact that the overhead light was on because Max couldn't sleep in the dark, and it made for what was probably the worst night's sleep I've ever had.

128

As soon as the sun popped its head over the horizon, I quietly clambered down the ladder and tiptoed past my sleeping cousins.

Out in the hall, I drew in a few deep breaths, clearing my lungs of Max's toxic gas, then headed downstairs for an early breakfast. Having a bit of time before the rest of the family got up would give me a chance to test if my ability to lie had come back. If it hadn't, I'd also have time to cry uncontrollably for a good hour or so before anyone else woke up.

Or so I thought.

"What are you doing here?" I asked, gently closing the living-room door behind me.

Jodie looked up from the table at the far end of the room and swallowed a mouthful of cornflakes. "Eating breakfast. What does it look like?"

What it looked like was some kind of ghostly apparition. Jodie's hair was a tangled rat's nest and her face was as pale as the milk in her bowl. Her eyes were bloodshot, with dark circles round them.

I cleared my throat. Now was my chance to lie. I'd tell her how good she looked and – *boom!* – Beaky Malone would be back in the game.

"You look like a zombie panda," I said.

Clearly not back in the game yet, then…

"Is it any wonder?" Jodie snapped. "I was stuck sleeping on the floor again."

"I bet you slept better than I did," I muttered, grabbing a bowl and taking a seat across from her.

Under the table, Destructo gave a grunt, licked my foot once, then went back to sleep.

I tipped some cereal into the bowl, then sloshed on some milk. "How were Mum and Dad after I went to bed?" I asked.

"Not happy."

I crunched on the cornflakes. "How not happy?"

"*Very* not happy."

"*Grounded* not happy?"

"Grounded *for a month* not happy."

I swallowed the cereal. "But it wasn't my fault. I couldn't help it," I protested. "We have to make them believe us about the machine."

Jodie shook her head. "They weren't buying it. I tried, Beaky, but we're on our own."

"We should go and look for the shop today," I suggested. "I can't go through school tomorrow telling the truth all the time. I'll be killed."

Jodie swirled her cereal with her spoon. "We could do that. We definitely *could* do that, or…"

"Or what?"

"Or we could just enjoy it for a bit."

I gaped at her. "Enjoy it? How can I enjoy it? It's torture."

"Oh no, I don't mean for *you* to enjoy it," Jodie grinned. She leaned closer to me across the table. "I mean me. Lying awake all night gives you plenty of time to think, and what I thought was, 'Wouldn't it be nice to embarrass Beaky as much as he's embarrassed me over the years?'"

She leaned back again, but her grin stayed fixed in place. "Like the time you announced on the radio that I liked to eat from the bins. Or the time you phoned the school and told the office to put out an announcement that I had to go home and collect my incontinence pants."

Despite everything, I couldn't help but chuckle. "Yeah, that was good."

"Not for me, it wasn't," Jodie scowled. "So, like I say, I think we should take some time to enjoy this new direction of yours."

She reached across the table to where Dad had abandoned his notebook and pen, then flipped to a new page.

"Now, where shall we start?" she wondered out loud. "Any embarrassing secrets, Beaky?"

I fought against it, but the word forced its way out. "Loads."

Jodie's eyes lit up. "Aha!" She clicked the button that made the point of the pen pop out. "Begin."

"N-no," I stammered, but I could already tell I was fighting a losing battle.

I tried to get up from the table, but Jodie clamped a hand on my arm. She stared at me, the pen hovering over the empty page. My jaw ached from trying to keep my mouth shut. I felt the words well up inside me like a bubble.

"I'm terrified of kittens, I'm the one who made that big dent in the car last month, and I quite fancy Miss Gavistock the dinner lady."

Jodie guffawed with laughter. "Excellent. Anything else?"

My tongue wrestled with the word, trying to pin it down, but the need to tell the truth was too great. "Yes!"

"Great! Go on, then…"

Before I could reply, there was a sound from the front door. We both looked round in time to see the letterbox opening and the end of a rolled-up newspaper being shoved through. It was a Sunday paper and the thick supplements made the whole thing get jammed halfway through the slot.

"Paperboy," I said, then I felt my pulse quicken. The paperboy! Yes! This could be my escape.

Leaping up from the table, I raced to the door and yanked it open. A lanky teenage boy drew back in surprise at the sight of me smiling broadly at him in my pyjamas.

"Uh, hi," he muttered.

"Hello!" I beamed, turning just in time to see Jodie throw herself to the floor behind the sofa. "It's Adam, isn't it?" I said.

Adam nodded. "That's right. You're Jodie's

brother, Beaky, aren't you?"

"Bingo! Got it in one," I said. I raised my voice, making sure Jodie heard. "Did you know that my sister has a massive crush on you?"

From behind the sofa, I heard Jodie give a sharp intake of breath.

"Uh, no. I didn't know that," Adam said.

"Oh, well, she very much does," I said. "She has a top-five list of boys she likes, and you, Adam, are in a very respectable third place. She's even written your name and hers together in a big heart and coloured it in. It's in her homework diary. It's really quite artistic."

Adam didn't seem to know what to do with this information. He blushed slightly and smiled at the same time. "Um, that's cool."

"Would you like to know who else is on the list?" I asked, before Jodie slammed into me at high speed, knocking me to the ground.

I squirmed and struggled, but Jodie was on top of me, pinning me down with one hand while clamping the other over my mouth. With her crazy hair and bloodshot eyes she looked like some sort of wild jungle woman. Adam's jaw dropped as he caught sight of her.

"Ignore him," Jodie said to Adam, then she glanced down at her pyjamas, remembering the state she was in. She hooked the door with her foot. "I'm not looking my best," she said, then she slammed the door in Adam's face.

A moment later, the newspaper plopped on to the mat. Jodie waited until she heard the gate close, then turned to me, eyes blazing.

"You read my diary," she growled.

"I didn't," I said, in all honesty. That took her by surprise.

She searched my face. "You're lying."

"I can't lie, remember?" I said. "I technically have not read a single page of your diary, I promise."

Her eyes narrowed. "What do you mean, *technically*?"

"I photocopied it," I explained. "And then I read that. Twice."

I braced myself, waiting for her to slap, punch, twist, nip or gouge at some part of me. Instead, she just stared at me in horror, then jumped up and ran out of the room. A moment later, I heard the bathroom door slam shut upstairs.

Standing, I dusted myself down, then went back to the dining table to finish my breakfast. "That showed her," I said, stuffing cereal into my mouth.

Jodie completely deserved her humiliation. She had been gathering ammunition to do even worse to me. So why did I feel so bad? Had she just hit me, that would have been fine, but she'd seemed more upset than angry as she'd legged it out of the room.

Swallowing the cereal, I pushed the bowl away and went to check on her. Climbing the stairs, I tapped gently on the bathroom door. "Jodie? Are you OK?"

"Go away, Beaky," came her voice from the other side of the door.

"I'm worried about you," I said, then added, "also, I'd like you to get out of the bathroom so I can have a quick poo before anyone else wakes up."

Beaky's Poo Plan

"What's going on?" asked Aunt Jas, appearing on the landing behind me.

Drat. So much for my poo plan.

"It's Jodie. She's locked herself in the bathroom," I explained.

Aunt Jas scratched her head. Only one of her eyes seemed to be working. I guessed she wasn't used to 6 a.m. wake-up calls. "Why has she done that?"

"Because Beaky has ruined my life," said Jodie through the door.

"She's exaggerating," I said. "All I did was tell a boy that she has a crush on him and four other boys in school, then reveal that I photocopied her diary and read it all twice. She's completely overreacting."

Mum staggered out of her bedroom. "What's going on? What time is it?"

"Jodie's locked herself in the bathroom," Aunt Jas said. "Dylan's ruined her life, apparently."

"And he dented the car last month," added the voice from the bathroom.

"He did *what*?"

"Morning, Mum," I said cheerfully. "Sleep well?"

It was clear from the way Mum glared at me that she still wasn't happy. She pushed past me and tried the bathroom door handle. "OK, Jodie, open up," she said. "I need to use the bathroom."

"He made me look like an idiot in front of Adam," Jodie said.

Mum turned to me. "Which one's Adam?" she asked.

"The paperboy."

Mum rolled her eyes. "Not the skinny one with the teeth?" she whispered. "Oh, who cares what he thinks, sweetheart?" she said, raising her voice. "There are plenty more fish in the sea."

"You've got at least four of them on your list," I added, trying to be helpful.

The door flew open and Jodie dived at me. I yelped and dodged out of her path, then made a run for my bedroom.

"Get back here, Beaky," Jodie shouted, grabbing at me. "I'm going to kill you!"

Reaching my room, I pulled open the door, only to find Sophie standing on the other side, staring. The sound that escaped my lips was a high-pitched squeal of shock, but it soon turned into a cry of pain as Jodie slammed into me for the second time that day, pinning me to the floor.

Aunt Jas and Mum watched as Jodie pinched, nipped and jabbed at me.

"Should we help him?" Jas asked.

Mum yawned and shrugged. "Nah. They do this a lot."

They watched us for a little while longer. "Fair enough," said Jas, as Jodie pulled my ear with one hand while twisting my nose with the other. "In that case, I'll stick the kettle on."

CHAPTER 10

THE HIGH WIRE

Theo looked at Jodie. He looked at me. He looked back at Jodie again.

"Sorry, I'm still not getting it," he said, shaking his head. "What happened?"

Jodie sighed. We were halfway up a tall flight of wooden steps at the high-wire adventure centre, waiting for our turn. You could see the car park from up here. I could just make out Destructo in the back seat of our car. Aunt Jas had refused to let him into hers again, and we didn't dare risk leaving him in the house by himself, so we'd had to take both cars to stop him eating the telly.

The rest of the family were playing it safe on the kid-friendly course, leaving Jodie and me to tackle the big one.

Under orders from Jodie, I'd texted Theo before we'd left home and told him to meet us at the centre. After what had happened with Adam, Jodie wanted me back to normal fast, and she thought Theo might be able to help.

She explained everything again, from Madame Shirley's shop right up to the present (although she did miss out the bit with Adam, I noticed). The more she spoke, the more Theo's frown deepened.

"So … what are you saying?" Theo asked, when Jodie had finished. "That Beaky can't tell a lie?"

"Good grief," Jodie sighed. "Yes! That's exactly what I'm saying."

"I told you that by text yesterday," I reminded him. "You called me a weirdo!"

The queue moved up a step and we all did the same. Theo looked me up and down. "Nah," he said.

"It's true!" Jodie protested. "Ask him a question. Anything. Ask him anything."

Theo thought. "What's seven times four?" he said.

Jodie rolled her eyes. "Not that sort of question!"

"You said ask him anything," Theo grumbled.

The queue moved again. There were only six people between us and the top now.

"Ask him about something he's done or, I don't know, a secret or something. Not the times table."

Theo thought again, more carefully this time. He glanced nervously at Jodie before asking his question. "Were you really asked to go to the North Pole?"

I shook my head. "No."

"Does jam really make dogs explode?"

"No."

"Do you really fancy Miss Gavistock from the canteen?"

"Yes," I confessed. "That woman's an angel."

Jodie smiled triumphantly. "Is that evidence enough?"

"Well, no, not really," Theo said. "You could both still be winding me up. But I can't think of anything else to ask, so I'll take your word for it."

"Good. Then you can help us figure out how to fix him," Jodie said. "Before he completely ruins my life once and for all, if he hasn't done already."

We took another step up and arrived at the top of the stairs. Jodie's face fell as she spotted the staff member in charge. It was Daniel Tallon, the current number two in her top-five list of boys she'd most like to smooch.

"Hey, Jodes," he said, brushing back his long, flowing hair and showing off some almost-flawless teeth. "What are you doing here?"

Jodie tore her eyes from him long enough to shoot me a sideways look. I smiled broadly back at her and winked.

Jodie's jaw flapped open and closed as she turned back to Daniel. "Yes," she said, a little too loudly.

A frown flickered briefly across Daniel's nearly-but-not-quite perfect forehead. "OK, then," he said. He held up a harness. "Who's going first?"

"Yes," Jodie said again. "I mean, um, Beaky. You can go first."

Jodie shot me one of her Looks. Her face was a shade of red I'd never seen before, like a traffic cone with sunburn. Having already suffered one beating at her hands  today, I wasn't in a hurry to receive a second one. As Daniel fastened the harness round my legs, I smiled at Jodie and mimed zipping my mouth shut.

"OK, step up to the edge," Daniel said. He held out another harness to Jodie. "Put your leg in there, Jodes," he said.

It was clear to see that Jodie was getting in a real flap, thanks largely to Daniel's dazzling smile. She stared at the harness in confusion for several seconds, then lifted the wrong leg.

"Other one," he said. He took her leg and guided it into the harness. "Here, let me help."

Jodie's eyes widened. Her mouth began to break dance, unable to decide whether to smile, frown, gasp or do all three at once. In the end she pulled a sort of grimace which made her look like she was having a particularly tricky bowel movement.

While Theo was getting into his harness, I made the mistake of looking down. We'd been so caught up in our conversation that I hadn't noticed how high we were. The platform we stood on was right up among the treetops, and the ground was a dizzyingly long way away.

As I looked, the forest floor seemed to move in and out like the slider of a trombone. It rolled like waves. It spun like a top. It did other things I can't even describe, but which were really quite unpleasant to look at and made my insides turn to jelly.

"There's a very good chance I'm going to soil myself," I whispered.

Daniel grinned and slapped me on the back. "There's nothing to it," he said. "On this first obstacle you just step off and swing to the next platform. Simple."

"Oh, I just step off, do I? Into empty space?" I replied, suddenly finding it tricky to breathe. "That's easy for you to say. This is scarier than kittens."

Daniel glanced over to Jodie. She smiled awkwardly. "Don't worry about him. He's got this thing going on where he tells the truth all the time. It's pretty funny, actually."

I raised an eyebrow. "Oh, me telling the truth's

funny, is it?" I said, turning to Daniel. "Here's one for you then, Daniel. This'll make you laugh. Jodie has this list in her diary—"

With one big shove, Jodie pushed me off the platform. My stomach shot up to my ears as my feet left the solid wood and dropped into empty space. Flapping my arms, I desperately tried to fly, but without much success.

The rope went tight, jerking me violently. I clung to it with both hands and looked up. The rope was making a worryingly high-pitched sound as it swung me across the gap. At first, I thought it was going to snap, then I realized the high-pitched sound was actually me, screaming as I hurtled through the air like an out-of-control Tarzan.

Aieeeeeee!

The net on the other side took me by surprise. I hit it with an *oof*, then scrabbled frantically to grab hold. With a final gasp, I hauled myself up on to the next platform.

Shaking, I turned back to the others. I could see Jodie laughing on the other side of the gap. Theo gave me a thumbs up, but even he was grinning a bit too broadly for my liking.

"I didn't soil myself, but I did come dangerously close," I shouted across the gap, which made everyone on the platform –

including complete strangers – crease up. "I didn't mean to say that out loud," I added, which just made them laugh even harder.

This was torture! Everyone was laughing at me, and if I didn't find a way to start lying again, people would be laughing at me *forever*.

Turning away, I folded my arms and scowled. Enough was enough. I had to put an end to this truth-telling nonsense once and for all, and desperate times called for desperate measures.

"Are you sure this is a good idea?" said Theo.

We had finished the high wire, and were now sneaking through the indoor staff-only section of the centre, searching for the manager's office.

"Yes," I whispered. "I've got a plan."

"But is it a good plan?" Jodie asked.

I shook my head. "Not really," I admitted. "But it's all I could come up with, and since you two couldn't think of anything, it's the only plan we've got."

The plan was pretty simple. I was going to humiliate myself into lying. In order for me to embarrass myself on a big enough scale, though, there was one thing I needed.

"There," I said, as we found the manager's office.

We ducked round a corner, keeping out of sight.

"Now what?" asked Theo.

"Now one of you has to go and convince—" I glanced at the door – "Tim Hughes, to leave his office."

Theo and Jodie exchanged a puzzled look.

"Why us?" Jodie asked.

"Well, I can't very well do it, can I?" I reminded her. "I'd march up there, knock on the door and tell him the entire plan."

"So, you *really* can't lie?" said Theo.

I tutted. "Theo, you're my best friend and I like you a lot but, wow, you're slow sometimes. No, I can't lie. Now, someone get the manager out of his office."

"Fine. I'll do it," huffed Jodie.

Theo and I hung back. We listened to her shuffle nervously up to the door, then knock.

The door opened. A surprised voice said, "Yes?

What are you doing here? It's staff only."

"It's … there's… I mean, the thing is…" Jodie fumbled. I rolled my eyes. What an amateur.

"There's a woman demanding to see the manager," she finally blurted. "I think she's from Environmental Health. Daniel Tallon asked me to come and get you."

"Oh no, not Environmental Health again," the manager groaned. "They've never forgiven us for that baby getting stuck up the tree."

Theo and I ducked back as the manager rushed past our hiding place on his way to the main centre. When he was out of sight, we darted into the office with Jodie and closed the door behind us.

I scanned the room. There were dirty cups and chocolate wrappers on every surface. The desk groaned under stacks of paperwork, boxes of tickets and a plastic tub containing the congealed remains of what looked like a chicken tikka masala.

Where was it? Where was it?

Aha!

"Theo, lock the door," I said, lowering myself into the manager's chair. I pushed the papers and old curry aside and moved a little upright microphone into position in front of me.

There was no key in the lock, so Theo wedged the back of a wooden chair under the handle to stop anyone opening it.

"Now what?" Jodie asked.

"Simple," I said, pointing to the microphone. "This is the tannoy system. Anything I say into this will be amplified through dozens of speakers all over the centre. Everyone here – hundreds of people – will hear every word I say."

"So?" said Theo.

"So, you two are going to ask me the most

embarrassingly cringe-worthy questions you can think of, and I'm going to answer them."

"Why would you deliberately humiliate yourself?" said Jodie.

"I wouldn't! That's the beauty of it. There's no way I'd deliberately broadcast embarrassing stuff about myself for everyone to hear," I said. "I'm sure my lying muscles will kick in to save me. They've got to."

Theo shuffled from foot to foot. "Sounds risky."

"It is," I agreed. "That's why it's going to work."

"This? This is your plan?" Jodie scowled.

"It is. And like I said, it's the only one we've got, so if you're both ready, let's begin."

And with that, I twiddled the button to turn on the tannoy system. Then, using a letter opener from the manager's desk tidy, I broke off the button and pinged it to the other side of the room.

CHAPTER 11

REVELATIONS

"Attention, everyone. My name is Dylan Malone," I announced. "Although most people call me Beaky on account of my nose being massive."

"Finally, he admits it," Jodie muttered.

"Please listen to the following announcement," I continued. I could just hear my voice echoing through the speakers out in the park, and imagined everyone stopping to listen. I looked at Theo and Jodie and gave them an encouraging nod.

They glanced at each other, then at me, then at the floor, searching for something to say.

"Well, come on," I urged. "Ask me something."

"Can't think of anything," whispered Theo. Great. Some help he was.

I turned to Jodie, but her expression was as blank as Theo's. "Come on, you had plenty to ask me this morning. Now's your chance!"

Jodie shrugged slowly. "Um … tell us your most embarrassing secrets."

Technically, that wasn't even a question, but it was enough to do the trick. I could feel my brain stirring, the words lining up to blurt themselves into the microphone and shame me forever.

How many people in the park would know me? How many kids from my school would be there? Ten? Twenty? There was no way my brain would let me completely humiliate myself. No way.

"I like to pull bits of hard skin off my feet and chew them," I said.

My whole body tensed. *No!*

"It's delicious," I added.

No, no, no, no, no!

Frantically, I scrabbled to turn off the tannoy, but without the button it was stuck on. I bit my lip, trying to stop the words coming out, but it was pointless. What had I been thinking? This was the worst plan in the history of mankind.

"Sometimes, I like to fart on my own hand then smell it," I babbled.

Theo and Jodie were just staring at me now, their eyes like saucers. I tried to stand up, but my Madame-Shirley-scrambled-brain was having none of it.

I gritted my teeth and felt my face turn red with the effort of keeping the words from escaping. My fingertips gripped the edge of the desk until my knuckles turned white.

"He's going to burst! We have to help him," Theo gasped. He shot a look at my sister, then sidestepped out of her reach. "Beaky! What are Jodie's biggest secrets?"

"What?" Jodie yelped.

Yes! Thank you, Theo!

"She got her bellybutton pierced even though Mum told her not to. She's got a top-five list of boys she fancies, including Daniel who works here. She drew a picture of them all mashed together like Frankenstein's monster. It was disturbing on a number of levels…"

"Tell me embarrassing stuff about Theo," Jodie barked. I shot my friend an apologetic look as my mouth started moving all on its own.

"He picks his nose and eats it. His mum once bought him girls' pants by mistake, but he wore them anyway."

"They were very comfortable!" Theo protested. "Tell us something else. Anything. Tell us a secret about someone you know."

"Not us," Jodie said.

A jumble of words swirled around in my head. There was no point resisting. My mouth opened.

"Last night, Steve kept talking about another woman in his sleep, not Aunt Jas."

Jodie gasped. Even Theo looked shocked.

With a single tug, Jodie pulled the wire out of the back of the microphone, and a brief screech of feedback echoed across the park.

The words stopped swirling in my head. I flopped back in the manager's chair and smiled weakly at Jodie and Theo. "So…" I began. "Do you think anyone heard any of that?"

Unsurprisingly, it turned out that everyone had heard everything I'd said, thanks to the wonders of tannoy technology.

We'd ducked out of the room just seconds before the manager had come storming back in, and – despite my better judgement – had gone to find Mum, Dad and the others.

We finally tracked them down in the café. Mum and Dad were sitting across a table from an ashen-faced Steve. Aunt Jas and the kids were nowhere to be seen.

Mum's face darkened as she saw us approaching. "Get here now," she said, pointing to a space on the bench beside her.

Cautiously, I sat down. "And you," Mum said to Jodie. Jodie joined me on the bench. Steve still hadn't looked up from the table.

"Nice to see you, Theo," said Dad. "Probably best you shoot off, eh?"

Theo almost cheered with relief. "Great!" he said. "Um, I mean... I'll see you at school, Beaky."

With a supportive glance my way, Theo made a mad dash for freedom.

"What were you *thinking*?" Dad demanded.

"Dan, please. Let me handle this," said Mum. She turned to me. "What were you *thinking*?"

"I just... I just wanted to be able to lie," I said. "That's not too much to ask, is it?"

Mum shook her head. "Not this nonsense again. Obviously you can lie just fine. You're doing it now."

"I'm not!" I protested. "There really was a magic box or ... something. It's the truth. I really can't lie."

"He is telling the truth," Jodie said, but a look from Mum stopped her saying any more.

Steve looked up at me. For a change, he wasn't wearing his sunglasses, and I could see his tired-looking eyes. "I wouldn't talk about another woman in my sleep," he said.

"But ... but you did," I insisted. "You kept saying you loved her, and that you wanted to be with her forever

and some

other

romantic

guff!"

Steve looked

taken aback. "I did? What was her name?"

Everyone watched me expectantly. I felt myself wilt beneath their gaze. "I ... can't remember," I admitted. "It was an unusual name, though. Definitely not Jas."

"Where is Jas?" Jodie asked, looking around.

"She and the kids went back to the house after Dylan's little announcement," Mum said. "To pack."

"Pack?" I said. "You don't mean...?"

Steve nodded and put his sunglasses back on, hiding his eyes. "Yeah," he said, his voice cracking. "She broke up with me."

Jodie stood up. "This is all that machine's fault," she said. "That shop. I dragged Beaky into that shop." She gasped. "It's *my* fault!"

"What are you talking about?" asked Dad.

Jodie caught me by the arm. "Doesn't matter," she said. "I'm going to sort it. We'll meet you at home, OK?"

"Get back here," said Mum, as Jodie pulled me away from the table. "I'm not finished with you two yet."

"Sorry, Mum," said Jodie, pushing me out of the café. "I need to fix Beaky before he does any more damage!"

As we dashed out of the café, we almost ran straight into Daniel. He smiled his runner-up smile.

"Hey, Jodes. So … Frankenstein's monster, eh? What part was I?" he asked, but Jodie barged past him, shoving him aside.

"Not now," she snapped.

"The hair and one of the eyes," I called back over my shoulder, as my sister dragged me towards the bus stop out front. "And three of the fingers on the left hand."

A short bus ride and a long walk later, we were standing on the spot we both agreed Madame Shirley's Marvellous Emporium of Peculiarities should be. Across the street was the same furniture shop we'd passed several times the day before, only this time it was closed.

Madame Shirley's shop wasn't closed, though, it was just … gone. There was a dusty *To Let* sign in the window, and a pile of mail scattered on the mat inside the door. From the look of the envelopes, it had all been there for a while.

I would have said there was no way this could possibly have been the same shop, were it not for one tiny detail. There, right in the middle of the bare wooden floor, was a single packet of pickled onion crisps.

"It's not here," I said.

"How can it not be here?" Jodie wondered. "She can't have moved out overnight."

"I don't think she did," I said. "I think she moved out yesterday, right after we left. That's why we couldn't find the shop."

Jodie snorted. "That's impossible."

"Yeah," I agreed. "As impossible as a metal box that makes people tell the truth."

"Fair point," Jodie conceded. "I wish we'd never seen that stupid shop."

I blinked. "Jasmine," I muttered.

Jodie frowned. "What?"

"Jasmine," I said, a memory flickering at the back of my mind. "You said you wished we hadn't seen the shop."

"So?"

"So... You wished. Wishes. Genie. Magic lamp. Aladdin," I said.

Jodie looked me up and down. "Are you having some sort of breakdown?"

"No! It reminded me! Aladdin. Princess Jasmine."

"Beaky, what are you talking about?" Jodie demanded, grabbing me by the shoulders.

"Jasmine! That was the name Steve kept

168

mentioning in his sleep. That's the woman he's secretly in love with."

Jodie stared at me. Her fingers dug into my shoulders and her teeth clamped together. "You *idiot*," she hissed.

"What have I done now?" I asked, squirming against her death-grip.

"What do you think 'Jas' is short for?"

Oh.

Oh *right*.

Suddenly Steve's night-time ramblings made much more sense.

"I didn't think it was short for anything," I admitted. "But, if I had to choose, I'd probably have said 'Jasper'."

"Aunt Jasper?" Jodie yelled. "You thought her name was Aunt *Jasper*?"

Giving me one final shake, Jodie about-turned

and ran back in the direction of the bus stop. "Come on, we have to get home," she said.

I looked back at the empty shop. "But what about me? What about fixing me?"

"Sorry, Beaky, but we've got to try and fix Jas and Steve first," Jodie said. "I just hope we're not too late."

CHAPTER 12

THE CHASE

We were too late. Jas and Steve were driving away as we ran the final few dozen metres home. Jodie and I stumbled to a stop and bent over, panting and wheezing. Through the taped-on back windscreen, I saw Max and Sophie both give us a sad wave.

"Where have you two been?" Mum demanded from the doorstep.

"Doesn't matter," Jodie gasped. "Where are they going?"

"Home," Mum said. "They're going home, then Steve is going to pack his bags."

Dad stepped up behind Mum and put a hand on her shoulder. "Maybe they'll work it out."

"You saw Jas," Mum said, shaking her head. "I think it's over."

"No!" Jodie cried. "We need to talk to them."

"We have to go after them," I said. "Dad, get the car, we can still catch up."

Mum sighed. "Not more games, Dylan."

"Look, there's no time to explain," I said, raising my voice. "I can fix this. Aunt Jas and Steve, I can fix it."

I met Mum's eye. "But you're going to have to trust me," I added.

Dad put his hands on his hips. "I don't know, Dylan, you've been—"

"*Dad!*" Jodie snapped, so loudly that we all jumped. "Get the car," she ordered. "Now!"

Dad yanked the wheel left, swerving just in time to avoid a van coming the other way. Its horn blared angrily as it sped by.

"This is exciting, isn't it?" said Dad, flooring the accelerator.

Mum grabbed the handle above the door and braced the other hand against the dashboard. "That's one way of putting it," she murmured.

Dad crunched down a gear and merged on to the dual carriageway. Jodie had her phone pressed to her ear. "Jas still isn't answering," she said.

"Keep trying," I instructed.

"I've been trying for fifteen minutes. She's not going to pick up," Jodie said, but she hit redial and tried again.

Another horn blasted from behind us as Dad switched lanes suddenly. "It's an emergency!" he shouted into the rear-view mirror, then he grinned from ear to ear. "It's like being in an action movie, this. Oh! It's just given me an idea for a jingle."

He took a deep breath. **"Iffffff youuuuu're driving in a hurry and your wife begins to worry—"**

"There!" I cried, pointing ahead. Aunt Jas's car was trundling along, a dozen vehicles or so in front of us, the back windscreen rattling with every bump in the road.

Dad pushed down on the accelerator. The car complained noisily, but gradually began to speed up. "Closing in on target," Dad said in a robotic voice. He was loving every minute of this.

A minute or two later, we were right behind Jas's car. "Get their attention," said Mum, leaning over and blocking Dad's view of the road. She pulled a lever at random and the windscreen wipers swooshed across the screen.

"What are you doing? I can't see!" Dad protested, straining to look over her head.

"I don't think they're noticing the windscreen wipers," I said.

"I thought it was the lights," Mum tutted. "Forget it. Let's try this."

She pushed the centre of the steering wheel and the horn squealed. Jas's car swerved briefly, then we saw Sophie and Max's faces through the glass.

We waved at them, then Mum pointed to the side of the road, indicating they should pull over.

A few seconds later, Aunt Jas's indicator started to blink. She changed lanes, then turned off on to a worryingly familiar side road.

"Oh, it's Piddington Castle," Dad said, following Jas past the castle sign. He shot me a doubting look. "I wonder if they've got that gas leak fixed."

"Probably," said Jodie, before I could say anything. I gave her a grateful nod, then threw open the door as Dad brought the car to a stop in the car park.

Aunt Jas, Steve and the kids were already out of their car. They looked confused as I ran up.

"Jas, I made a mistake," I blurted. "What I said about Steve, it wasn't true."

"I knew it!" cheered Steve, punching the air. He held open his arms to Jas. "C'mere, cutie-smoosh."

Jas gave him the cold shoulder. "So you were lying, Dylan? Why would you lie about something like that?"

"No, I wasn't lying," I said. "I can't lie, like I keep telling everyone, but nobody seems to believe me."

Jas crossed her arms. "So … you weren't lying? He was talking about a woman, then."

"Yes!" I said. "He was."

Behind me, I heard Mum take a step closer to Jodie. "How is this meant to be helping, exactly?"

"He went on and on about her all night. About how beautiful she was. About how much he adored her. I didn't get a wink of sleep," I explained. "He just wouldn't stop banging on about her."

Aunt Jas dabbed at the corner of her eye and sniffed. "That's enough, Dylan. I don't want to hear any more."

"No, but you have to," I said. "Because by the early hours of this morning I knew beyond any shadow of a doubt that Steve was completely, one-hundred-per cent in love with this woman."

Aunt Jas's face had gone strangely tight. "Get in the car, kids," she said, not even looking at Steve. "We're going home."

Mum and Dad both stepped forward and grabbed me. Dad clamped a hand over my mouth.

"Stop it, Dylan," he yelled.

"Sorry, Jas," Mum said. "He said he could help."

"He can!" Jodie cried. "Let him finish."

I struggled and squirmed. Dad's grip was too tight. There was nothing else for it.

"Yeeowch!" he yelped, whipping his hand away. "He bit my finger!"

"Wait!" I said, pulling free of Mum and Dad's grasp. "There was one other thing he said that you have to hear. It's really important."

With a resigned sigh, Jas looked at me. "What?"

"He said, 'Jasmine, will you marry me?'"

Tears sprang to Aunt Jas's eyes. "Jasmine?" she breathed.

"Beaky thought it was someone else. He thought your name was Jasper," said Jodie, joining me.

"Aunt *Jasper*?" snorted Dad. He shook his head. "We've raised an idiot."

"Hush, Dan," scolded Mum, elbowing him.

Jas looked over at Steve. He took off his sunglasses and we saw that he had tears in his eyes, too. The whole thing was so schmaltzy I sort of wanted to be sick in my mouth, but at the same time it was, I dunno, kind of nice.

"You said all that about me?" said Jas.

Steve shrugged. "Apparently," he said. "I mean... Uh, yes. Who else would I be talking about?"

With a glance over at us, Steve took a steadying breath, then lowered himself on to one knee. "Beaky sort of beat me to it, but ... Jasmine, will you marry me?"

Aunt Jas half smiled and half cried, making a

bubble of snot pop out of one of her nostrils, but I bit my lip and resisted the urge to announce it.

"Let me sleep on it," Jas said with a smirk. "And I'll tell you in the morning."

She bent down and gave Steve a hug. Max and Sophie ran to join in.

"Aw, that's nice," I said, watching them. Through a gap in their tangle of arms, I saw Sophie staring at me. "And a bit creepy," I added.

"Oi! You lot!"

Everyone turned in time to see a grey-haired castle guide hurrying down the driveway towards us. I recognized him right away as the one Destructo had knocked over the day before.

"Um, we should probably go," I said, but the guide was already too close.

"Is there something the matter?" Dad asked.

"Something the matter? *Something the matter?*" wheezed the guide, struggling to get his breath back. "No, there's nothing the matter. I just wanted to shake this lad's hand."

He took my hand in his and shook it enthusiastically. "Thanks to you, we've had our busiest day of the season," he said, gesturing around at the car park. Now I thought about it, it did look much fuller than it had the day before.

"How is that thanks to me?" I asked.

"Didn't you see the papers? There were reports that a ghostly hound was spotted stalking the castle corridors," the guide said. He winked. "Folks have been coming from all over to try to catch a glimpse of it. There's even talk of them filming one of them ghost-spotting documentaries here next month."

The guide looked around. "Where is it, by the way?"

"Where's what?" asked Dad.

"The dog," said the guard.

I could have sworn I actually felt Dad's heart stop. His face went a deathly shade of pale as he spun to face the boot of the car.

"The dog," he whimpered. "We've left the dog at home."

"The telly!" yelped Mum. "Come on, move, move, move!"

Mum jumped in the car, then immediately jumped back out again. She raced over and gave Jas, Steve and the kids a hug. "Come back soon, OK?"

"We will," said Jas. "And Dylan ... thanks."

"Any time," I said, sliding into the back seat and closing the door. Just before we pulled away,

I wound down the window and pointed to Sophie. "But she still creeps me out."

"Me too, dude!" laughed Steve, before Jas slapped him on the arm.

The car tyres spun and we roared out of the car park, spraying chips of gravel behind us. I looked back in time to see 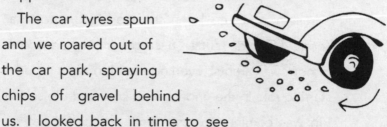 Jas and Steve taking each other by the hand. My truth-telling had come in useful, after all. Even if, technically, it had caused all the problems in the first place.

"You did good," said Jodie.

"Thanks," I said.

"We'll find Madame Shirley's place and get you turned back. I promise."

"No arguments from me," I said.

"Are you going to tell me what you did with the photocopies of my diary?" Jodie asked.

"Nope," I said, truthfully.

"Didn't think so."

We joined the dual carriageway and Dad raced for home. I looked out of the window, watching the scenery whizz by.

Yesterday, I had been the world's greatest liar. Today, I couldn't utter a single fib. I had school tomorrow. Parents' Evening was looming. I had a starring role in the end-of-term play and the school trip was coming up fast. What if I didn't get my ability to lie back before all that? What if I *never* did?

As we hurried home to try to stop our dog eating the TV, I reckoned that, one way or another, the next few weeks were going to be pretty interesting.

And boy, was I right.

Read on to find out what Beaky gets up to next!

BEAKY MALONE

WORST EVER SCHOOL TRIP

← the clown

the bully →

the boy → who can't lie

BARRY HUTCHISON

CHAPTER 1

THE PERMISSION SLIP

It had been ninety-two hours since I'd last told a lie.

Up till then, I'd been something of a lying expert. If they gave out black belts for telling fibs, I'd have been a seventh Dan master. All that changed, though, when I stepped inside a rusty metal box that turned out to be the world's only truth-telling machine. Without going into detail, I hadn't been able to utter a single untruth since.

It was Wednesday morning, and I'd survived two full days of school with only three light beatings from my classmates, two telling-offs from teachers, and one wedgie from Helga Morris in the year above. Everyone says you should always tell the truth, but it turns out that, when you do, it can get you into all sorts of trouble.

Who'd have thought that people would take such offence when you remark on their bad breath and body odour? Mr Lawson, our head teacher, didn't take it at all well. Mind you, he was giving an assembly at the time.

But my problem isn't just the inability to lie. Whatever that box did to me, it means I struggle to keep the truth in. It's like it's always there, waiting to come out at the worst possible times. I can be sitting quietly doing my work when I'll announce out of the blue that I'm planning on copying the person sitting next to me, or that I've just stuck a bogey under my desk.

Luckily, I sit next to my best mate, Theo, in most of my classes. Theo knows all about my lack of lying ability, and is great at helping me cover it up. He covers for me even though I've accidentally revealed pretty much every secret he's ever told me, including the one about him once drinking a whole carton of dog's milk. And quite enjoying it.

Anyway, like I was saying, it was Wednesday morning, and things were going surprisingly well – right up until the point the teacher, Mrs Dodds, peered at me over the top of her half-moon glasses.

"Ah, Dylan," she said. "I've got a bone to pick with you."

Everyone looked up from their work. All eyes went to the teacher, then to me. I shifted nervously in my seat. "Oh?" I asked innocently. "Is it about the time I wrapped your car in cling film?"

Mrs Dodds gasped and her eyes widened. "That was *you*? That took me hours to get off."

"Yes. And Theo," I said, jabbing a thumb in his direction. "He helped, too."

"Oh, thanks a bunch, Beaky," Theo muttered.

Mrs Dodds squinted at us both. "We'll discuss that later," she said, her voice ice cold. "What I was going to say was you haven't handed in your homework."

"Oh, that. Yeah. My dog ate it," I said.

The teacher sighed. "Your dog ate it? That's the best you could come up with, Dylan?"

"But it's true!" I protested. "My dog really did eat it."

"Dogs don't eat homework!" Mrs Dodds snapped.

"You've never met my dog," I told her. "He'll eat anything. Leave him alone with the TV too long and he'll have a go at eating that."

Some of the class sniggered at that, but I was being serious. Destructo was a Great Dane with an even greater appetite. He ate more food in a day than the rest of the family got through in a week, but was always scavenging for anything else he could gobble up. That included my homework, my pencils and, on one memorable occasion, my school bag.

"And what about your permission slip for the school trip?" Mrs Dodds asked, arching one of her bushy grey eyebrows. "I suppose the dog ate that, too?"

"No," I said, shaking my head. "My sister stuffed it into my mouth when I posted a picture of her toes on Instagram."

The teacher stared at me in silence.

"She's got really hairy toes," I explained. "Like a troll."

The class giggled. Mrs Dodds glanced round, clearly worried that the lesson was about to erupt into chaos, like it usually did.

"Quiet!" she snapped. "Get on with your work." She leaned forward in her chair, her hands clasped together on the desk. "I've never heard such nonsense in all my life, even from you, Dylan. You can pick up another form at the end of the lesson, but–" Her mouth curved into a thin smile – "it needs a parent to sign it, and if you don't get it back to me before the end of lunch, you can forget about going on the trip tomorrow."